JABBERWOCKY

JABBERWOCKY

Cui dono lepidum novum libellum?
—Catullus

PRIME BOOKS

TABLE OF. . .

Jabberwocky, *Lewis Carroll* 7
The Mummy Speaks, *Sarah Koplik* 9
Other Altars of the Heart, *Tim Pratt* 10
Shadowplay, *Sonya Taaffe*..........................13
Kikimora, *Ekaterina Sedia* 17
Song to the Selkie, *Gemma Files*.....................31
Silence, Before the Horn, *Marie Brennan* 33
Old Storm Shadow, *Lila Garrott* 35
The Clairvoyant, Between Dark & Dream, *Mike Allen*.....37
Little Match Girl, *Yoon Ha Lee* 40
The Lass of Loch Royal, *Holly Phillips* 41
Lament for Alexander, *Shirl Sazynski* 54
Helen, *JoSelle Vanderhooft* 56
Nymphs Finding the Head of Orpheus,
                Theodora Goss....................64

...CONTENTS

Revulsion and the Beast, *Vera Nazarian* 65

Baskets Full of Gods, *Rio Le Moignan* 72

In the Name of... *Anna Tambour* 75

Mother is a Machine, *Catherynne M. Valente* 77

Inside the Tower, *Stephanie Burgis* 81

Black Dog Times, *Jane Yolen* 86

How to Bring Someone Back from the Dead,
                Veronica Schanoes 87

The Ice Puzzle, *Catherynne M. Valente* 93

Skull Vault, *Sarah Singleton* 99

Jolly Bonnet, *Andrew Bonia* 101

In Grandmother's House, *Ainsley Dicks* 103

Alderley Edge, *Elizabeth Wein* 113

She Undoes, *Greer Gilman* 114

My Six Months' Darkness, *Jeannelle M. Ferreira* 117

JABBERWOCKY

Copyright © 2005 by **Sean Wallace**.
Cover, *The Romance of Le Galion III*, by **Claude Manuel**.
Cover design copyright © 2005 by **Garry Nurrish**.

ACKNOWLEDGEMENTS: Jeff Vandermeer, with all my thanks, for the use of **Jabberwocky**; John Betancourt, for the chance; Garry Nurrish, for what he does best; and last, but not least of all, Sonya: *Cave! advocatus diaboli, alma mater, et dolor in natis—summa cum laude.*

The individual stories and poems
are copyrighted by their respective authors.

Prime Books
www.prime-books.com

JABBERWOCKY
LEWIS CARROLL

(from *Through the Looking-Glass and What Alice Found There,* 1872)

> `Twas brillig, and the slithy toves
> Did gyre and gimble in the wabe:
> All mimsy were the borogoves,
> And the mome raths outgrabe.
>
> "Beware the Jabberwock, my son!
> The jaws that bite, the claws that catch!
> Beware the Jubjub bird, and shun
> The frumious Bandersnatch!"
>
> He took his vorpal sword in hand:
> Long time the manxome foe he sought—
> So rested he by the Tumtum tree,
> And stood awhile in thought.
>
> And, as in uffish thought he stood,
> The Jabberwock, with eyes of flame,
> Came whiffling through the tulgey wood,
> And burbled as it came!

One, two! One, two! And through and through
The vorpal blade went snicker-snack!
He left it dead, and with its head
He went galumphing back.

"And, has thou slain the Jabberwock?
Come to my arms, my beamish boy!
O frabjous day! Callooh! Callay!'
He chortled in his joy.

`Twas brillig, and the slithy toves
Did gyre and gimble in the wabe;
All mimsy were the borogoves,
And the mome raths outgrabe.

THE MUMMY SPEAKS —
SARAH KOPLIK

Might I know
That unbearable lightness
Of flesh and blood
The weight of my skin
My shoulders shaking with it
Coughing until I come up for air
A breath, whispers,
And all would be well
Or crumple into emptiness
I will not choose
The pain of indecision
Blurs my straight path crooked
Warped within I reach outward for balance
Dreams flutter around my feet like fallen leaves
Brittle veins of color lined with decay
I am a dream
Crushing myself within my own hand
May my dust be of some use yet.

OTHER ALTARS OF THE HEART
TIM PRATT

I'm watching through your window again, my face
against the dirty glass, squinting inward to watch
your progression from love to loneliness to more
final dispositions, and you don't know I'm there.
You are kneeling before a skeleton strung
up on the wall, it is cast in metal, bones
sewn together with thin copper filaments,
arms crossed pharaoh-style over an empty
chest (I don't mean to think of the tin man
but I do; he should have been a sociopath
armed with woodaxe and wit). You are kissing
the feet of the metal man. Your shrine to Aphrodite

is shoved aside, candles burned up and broken, mirror
turned down (a rejection of vanity or self-
reflection?), blue jars spilling their freight of dried
flowers onto your dirty carpet. Your floor
is ankle-deep in shreds of lace and rabbit droppings,
and your broken-necked bunny is clotted with black
flies. There are strange stains on the walls and your terminal
neighbor is wailing in sustained pain from next

door. Love is not a goddess much at home here.
The metal man is a new diversion of the
soul, another god I drove you to. You used
to worship naked but now you are swathed in cotton

and wool, a thick black scarf stifling your hair,
and I grow nervous standing on the sill. You have
turned your will from capricious Venus to a muted
metal shape on the wall, and I imagine
thick dark chains and swaddling cocoons
and the ball gags that always so unnerved
you. I know this god, this is the lord of the vault
of the heart, and as I watch, you sear your many wounds,
your love's amputations, and close your chest tight.
The night is yours now, your mouth is full of silver
teeth and your nails are sharp, your smile is vacant
and winning and you are the bearer of heart's death,

as I have unwittingly been. You dress in leather
and you are supple as molten lead, you
are all hard angles under imagined softness.
I sink from your window, stepping down to the natural
gas tank, down to the weedy gravel pockmark of
your back yard. I hear the pounding wordless music
from the strip club across the street and confuse it
with the beat of my blood. I think of all

the altars that I've led you to. I hope I never meet you in a bar. You will scatter men like ashes burned in the blue heart of your sacrificial fire, constant, untended, without heat.

SHADOWPLAY
SONYA TAAFFE

I: Footprints

I stop casting a shadow when I step into your house. In the speckled mirror over the banister, tarnished as a pond in winter, I make no more impression than the settling of dust. I used to wash all the windows; I hung that wallpaper when the old sloughed in mildewed strips like a dead snake's skin, decay molting the skeleton like an armature of spined ivory from the outgrown flesh. You picked out the curtains. Under my feet, under thin sour-cherry carpet where once we wore off the nap with dancing—did I ever learn to waltz? Did you only make me think I did?—the old boards neither creak nor resist, nothing to acknowledge that I have weight, displacement, consequence in this realm that you have made entirely yours. Even the air has forgotten that once I breathed it out. But I look into the mirror as I pass, through sunlight weak as cold tea, old reflections trapped in disintegration beneath glass like leached amber; and I cannot find all the ways I once lived here, only all the ways I left.

II: Photographs

If you cut me out of your pictures, I could forgive you. Scissors to snapshots in the careful origami of revision, eviscerating memory as though anger, swallowed, could thicken to cancer; sorrow proliferate in the blood like a virus, seeding neurons and capillaries with headache and feverish remembrance; old love curdles, clots, produces heart attacks. We become surgeons of our past, paring necrosis from nostalgia, inserting fine plates of distance, stainless and plastic-pristine, catgut and staples across the bruised and soft and scarred places where we let ourselves touch. Fire chews to ash; rain pounds the remnants into mud. But these pictures, furred with neglect and sifting time, you have not harmed. Only I have faded, absence provoking absence, out from under the crook of your younger arm or the careless splash of sun somewhere we might have been happy. No water needed to wear me away: no slow erasure into the grave. As beautifully indifferent as a black hole, you only ever needed yourself.

III: Wax and Lighters

Dust hangs like grains of fool's gold, turning in the slow drafts. This house smells like the ragged end of November. Did I tell you the story of the wax crocodile, how it seized the scribe's wife's lover in its teeth and plunged into the reed-stalked river? Or the Thessalian witches, who would steal a man's face and tack down a mask of wax in its place? This material more malleable than flesh, to be shoved and sculpted and softened with a thumb: the stylus incises and effaces, candles liquefy and drip down off the table's edge. We used to set lights in all the rooms, on sills and shelves, until every night looked like Halloween, like living inside a jack-o'-lantern; when our shucked clothes twined together like helices and all my books interleaved with yours. The corpses of candles are smoke stains on the ceiling. This house blows through me like a cold breath, blowing out.

IV: Overexposure

I thought you smiled like the sun: brilliance and warmth and the beaming core of my day. And radiation. All my skin is your scars.

V: Terminus

Those are not my books on the table. Afternoon and autumn alike are a wash of preservation, honey and formaldehyde: embalming an alien strata from my own. I remember the rain stain trickled down the wall, not the gilt frame hung crooked on a wire above it; the broken ledge of mantel, not the chunk of hematite sliced across its blood-black grain; this glass I might have drunk from, but never that fistful of rose stalks dropped inside it. You nailed those herbs over the lintel. Sage and juniper, bitter mouthfuls of smoke; rowan twigs tangled in a handful of red thread. But I was never your devil, and you have not let me in: we neither of us could bear the touch of holy water now. This is my discarded flesh, fingers from scapulae, kneecaps from larynx, skull as hollow with chill dust as an attic, spine stranded from ribs. Wallet from keys, sweater from paperbacks, capped red pens like stripped phalanges, records scattered from rings. All the fragments of myself, disbanded, evaporated, and there is no box that contains my heart. If you were to raise your eyes to mine, even to curse me, I might reassemble like Ezekiel's clicking jackstraws in this dryest valley where once our words were rain, our fingers interlaced like rivers. If you were to touch me, even to wound, I might gather substance enough to be hurt. If you were to remember, I might even speak. But your feet are crossed by no shadow, your face is alone in the glass; light clarifies the air like a knife, and when you look back from the doorway, I am not there.

KIKIMORA
EKATERINA SEDIA

The fall of communism came about when I was in the middle of my PhD in astrophysics; the steel jaws of 1990 followed close behind. My hometown, a speck on the forested expanse of Siberia, felt its hungry bite. Even Novosibirsk, where I attended graduate school, careened into the cold, joyless chaos, buckled by that wolf-year. This was when I decided to move to Moscow, trying to escape the grey limbo.

"Looking for an easy life," they called it. I just wanted to be able to support myself; is that asking for too much? But there were no need for astrophysicists, and secretute jobs that were abundant did not appeal to me. I had to fall back on my gymnastic childhood, and started teaching aerobics to the tourists who stayed in Ukraina Hotel. There, through the gym window, I could see the river bend carving off the downtown from the rest of the city. And there I met Anya.

She was a maid with the master's degree in psychology. We ran into each other in the locker room—I was just getting ready for class, and she was cleaning the mirrors. I noticed her because of the way she was looking at me—not sizing up competition, but simply appraising. I introduced myself, and soon we were commiserating on the impossibility of finding a job in one's field.

We laughed at first, and then grew silent, contemplating the world in which an advanced degree was a requirement for a janitorial job. She was younger than I, but still she felt old and outdated in the scary, shifty-eyed world that was springing around us, the world with no past or future but only a slightly soiled present. Then we kissed.

I looked over her shoulder, to make sure that there was no one watching, and I saw a tall, dark-skinned man with deep green hair, who stood in the doorway. I jolted and pushed her away; she gave me a wounded look, and the stranger was gone.

"Marina?" She stared at me, puzzled and annoyed.

"Sorry," I said. "I thought there was someone at the door."

She smiled, and a hidden secret place seemed to have opened in her eyes, letting thorough a warm glow. Like a hearth. Like home. Protected from the cold river wind and uncertainty. "When are you getting off?"

"After 6 pm class. You?"

"At eight. You can wait for me, and come over if you want."

I nodded. "Where do you live?"

"Kozhukhovo."

It was a long trip to the suburbs, but I didn't mind. We held hands on the subway. Anya laughed.

"What?"

"Just funny. If we were men, can you imagine the looks we would've got?"

"Prejudice has its place," I murmured, sinking my face into the faux fur collar of her coat. Even the most opinionated old women did not seem to think that we were anything more than friends. It suited me fine—Anya's wispy hair was brushing against my forehead, and I breathed in the smell of her skin and the still-present aroma of mothballs from her coat. Out of the corner of my eye, half-closed in bliss, I saw the green-haired man again.

He stood holding onto the overhead rail, oblivious to my attention. Everyone in the subway car either ignored or did not notice him. At first, I guessed him for a Chechen, with his dark skin and an old-style Caucasus cloak, with its ostentatious shoulder pads. But no shoulder pads swept up so abruptly and vertically; the shape of the cloak suggested parts no human body had a right to possess. And the dark hue of his skin was imparted by neither sun nor ethnicity—it was the color of tree bark, furrowed by more than age. He swayed with the car, and his dark green hair shimmered and swayed too.

It occurred to me that he was supposed to have a green beard. At first, I could not puzzle out the source of this thought; then I realized that I had seen such a creature before. Deep within the Siberian woods, a forest spirit commonly known as a leshy.

I smiled at the green-haired stranger. The thought that there was something untouched by the present made living tolerable.

His moss-green eyes met mine, and a slow smile cracked the dark wood of his face. That smile made me feel like someone from home came to visit, bringing homemade preserves and letters from long-forgotten relatives.

"What are you looking at?" Anya whispered into my ear.

I knew better than to point at the leshy, and just shrugged. He got off at the next stop, and Anya's hand snuggled under my elbow.

I was glad to find out that even a place so cold and pedestrian as Moscow in November had its own spirits. After all, it used to be a forest once, and apparently its guardian leshy had endured longer than the trees.

Anya nudged me, and withdrew her soft hand from the comforting proximity of my breast. "We're here."

Anya lived with her parents and a grandmother. All of them seemed quite happy to meet me, and fed us supper of stuffed peppers, followed by several liters of tea. It was warm and homey three-room apartment, replete with a cat and a fish tank. I petted the cat who purred emphatically, and tried to ignore the kitchen-table conversation that centered on politics and inflation, like every conversation did those days. I kept glancing over to the window, where I could see the streetlamps reflected in black river water. I wondered if the granite-encased riverbank was home to rusalki.

The sound of Anya's name brought me back to the kitchen table.

"She's almost twenty-five," her grandmother lamented. "Only in a time like this, how're you supposed to find a man? All the good ones are barely making ends meet, and all the rich ones . . . " She stopped, her wrinkled face expressing a great desire to spit. "Bandits and thieves."

"I know," I said. "I'm twenty-seven."

Anya's mother nodded sympathetically, and Anya drank her tea to conceal a fit of laughter.

I never told my parents about my sexual proclivities—I didn't want to complicate things; yet, I was mad at Anya. I felt dirty as they invited me to stay the night, promising to lay out an inflatable mattress in Anya's room. They wouldn't be so welcoming if they knew. I just didn't like taking advantage of their naiveté.

Anya kicked me under the table. I caught myself, trying to straighten out my facial expression—I knew that I was giving Anya what my grandmother called a 'wolf look.' Not pretty on a girl.

We waited until everyone was asleep, and giggled and made love in the dark, hushing each other and giggling more. It was still dark outside, but the quality of the darkness, the way it retreated around the streetlamps in the yard and the edges of the sky suggested that the morning was not far off. I returned to my inflatable mattress, leaving Anya to sigh in her sleep, but felt restless.

I perched on the windowsill. It started to snow, and I watched the fat snowflakes flutter through the cones of light cast by the streetlamps, and disappear into the darkness again. I was not surprised when I saw the leshy standing in one of the light cones, his hair encrusted in a translucent helm of melting snow.

"What do you want?" I whispered.

His answer resounded clear in my ears, as if he were standing next to me. "Come with me, and bring her along."

I glanced at Anya, who smiled in her sleep, the tabby cat curled up on her pillow.

"Yes, her."

"Why?"

"Trees need water to grow."

"What do you need me for?"

"You're a swamp thing, a green kikimora from a Siberian bog, an in-between place that bridges wood and rivers."

I huffed. I read enough children's stories to know that kikimoras were nasty, ugly things. "I'm certainly not a kikimora. Get bent." I slid off the windowsill and lay down, my heart beating against my ribs. I thought of the fairy tales, of everything I knew about leshys. They seemed malevolent more often than not—they could fool you, twist you around, make you lose your way in a forest. Only until now I never believed the stories.

I slept very little that night. My dreams were heavy, suffocating—I had no doubt that it was the leshy's doing. I dreamt of green slime covering my body, of tree bark growing over my skin, of the tree branches sprouting from my arms and legs. Of poisonous mushrooms in my underarms.

The leshy was apparently offended by my rudeness, and did not manifest himself for a while, except in dreams. Still, I tried to make sense of his words—forest and swamp and water, of his need, of how Anya fit into it. If she were the one he wanted, why didn't he show himself to her? Was I just an intermediary, or something greater? I could sense his presence in my dreams, deep and dark, tangled and permeated by the smell of the swamp.

In my waking life, I spent all my free time with Anya, and often could not wait to get out of my class to see her sweet dimpled face, to feel her soft hand in mine. And when she did not show up for work one day, my heart ached with a premonition of disaster. I called her at home, but no one there knew where she was.

I was a mad woman then, torn by grief and remorse, furious with my failure to ward off misfortune. I looked for Anya in every crowd, on every subway station, in the windows of every building I passed. I looked for her on the granite riverbanks, but the river was already encased in sickly green ice.

I looked for her in the ghostly-pale faces of rusalki, souls of drowned girls, their mouths gaping like underwater caves, their long, loose hair streaming and floating around their faces as if lifted by slow current. I found them under the bridge the night of the winter solstice. They did not shiver in their thin garments, and their eyes were remote and starless. They held hands and danced in a circle, their bare feet insensitive to the cold of the stone bank and of ice that encrusted it.

"Have you seen her?" I begged. "Did she drown?"

Their ethereal faces turned one pale cheek, then the other in a slow underwater no. "Not our sister," came their quiet, gurgling voices. "We've seen no girl falling through the ice; we've seen no girl struggling for air; we've seen no girl dragged into black, silent water. We've seen no new sister, and we dance without her."

I was somewhat comforted by their words. "Can you ask others?"

"Drowned puppies and alley cats haven't seen her either."

"Can you ask the leshy?"

They shook their heads in unison, their hair undulating like seaweeds. "Ask him yourself. You're an in-between one, a neither-here-nor-there . . . " Their voices trailed off, and they returned to their slow dance. They held hands and spun, sometimes on stone, sometimes on ice.

I stood and watched them, deaf and dumb from cold, darkness, and despair. They were long gone, and my feet grew numb, and the stars spilled over the sky like breadcrumbs on a table, when I regained my voice. I howled at the dark river, at the city nestled like an infant in the crook of its frozen elbow. I screamed for the leshy to come out, come out, wherever he was, and to give my Anya back. I knew that the bastard twisted her around, made her lose her way in the dark and the cold, to make me come for her.

No answer came, and I wondered away from the river, toward the boulevards that circled the heart of the city, studded with oversized jewels of frozen ponds, towards Alexandrovsky Garden. The streets were sleek with black ice that reflected the streetlights, as if there were another city hidden in frozen puddles. A façade of a three-story old mansion reflected there too, and its closed doors seemed open in its reflection. After a moment of hesitation, I closed my eyes and stepped into the upside-down maw of the reflected doorway.

For a moment, my foot touched the slippery solid surface of ice, and then broke through, into a faintly fluorescent, moldy air of an underground forest. Long beards of Icelandic moss hung from the rimed branches of dead spruces, and no footsteps resonated on a soft carpet of their fallen needles.

"Leshy," I called. "Give my girl back to me."

The wind rose and moaned and bent the treetops almost to the ground. The frozen whip of my hair lashed my face, and the hoarfrost in the air stung my eyes, narrowing them to rheumy slits.

"Come out, you bastard!"

I had no idea of where I was going in the underground dead

forest, screaming into the wind. I never questioned it, but let my guts lead me as long as my legs would carry me. Soon, buckled over by the wind, I sank to my knees in deep moss by a slender birch. It creaked and moaned under the assault of the wind. Yet, its bare branches bent over and around me, forming a protective cocoon, stroking my shoulders.

"Help me," I whispered.

The branches hugged me closer, and I felt rejuvenated and strong, as the dying tree poured the last of its life into me.

"I'm looking for a girl, as fair as your bark, as gentle as your touch. Have you seen her?"

The birch shuddered and stretched its branches against the howling storm, pointing deeper into the forest. I cringed as I heard a sharp crack of snapping wood. I thanked the birch and was on my way, plunging headlong into the solid wall of the wind.

I had no sense of direction, but the leshy was too eager to divert me: as much as he tried to confuse me, to make me lose my way, I kept turning into the wind, until I crossed a clearing and stood on the shore of a lake, its water calm despite the storm. Cattails fringed its shores, their leaves green and erect, their brown heads nodding to me as if in greeting. Yellow water lilies stood still over its mirror-clean surface; I realized how thirsty I was.

I drank on my knees, like an animal, the cool water soothing my cracked, burning lips, its water washing away the sting of the cold. I looked at the surface, waiting for it to calm down. I was expecting to see my face, but instead I saw Anya. The water caressed my fingers, and I recognized her despite her change.

A quiet fell over the world, and I could hear my labored breathing. And then, someone else's.

I turned around.

"So you've found her," the leshy said.

I nodded, and touched my fingers to the lake Anya's surface in reassurance. "I came to take her back."

The leshy smiled, and I noticed how much he'd aged since our last meeting. The bark of his skin seemed diseased, mottled with fungi, and the deep green of his hair was turning lichen-grey. "Take her back, eh? How are you going to accomplish that?"

I scrambled for an answer. If she were dead or unconscious, I would've gathered her into my arms and walked away. Were she turned to stone, I would've broken my back but carried her out. But she was liquid that poured over my fingers, streamed down my face, wetted my lips. "Turn her back to her human form," I said.

He smiled still. "I wish I could do that."

I raised my fist, furious with his smirk. "Don't play with me, or I'll smash your face in; I'll burn your forest, I'll salt the ground . . ."

He raised his palm. "Quiet, girl. I cannot do what you ask,

threaten all you want . . . I am not strong enough." He seemed embarrassed as he uttered the last words.

"Why not?"

"My forest is dying without water. I need you to bring it to the trees."

"And then you'll let us go?"

His steep shoulders slumped. "If that's what you wish, kikimora."

"Don't call me that!"

"I can call you whatever you wish me to, but it won't change what you are." His eyes were black holes, bottomless in the bark of his face; deep dark caverns, home to bats and night birds. "I need a swamp to bring the water to my trees; I need creeks and puddles, moss and bogs."

I sighed. "How do I do that?"

He gave me an apprehensive look, as if worried that I will swing at him again. "I'll help you along. Just be what you are."

And then I was. I unraveled and un-spun, my limbs splaying and elongating. My fingers twined with Anya's, watery and comforting. My skin split, exposing the hummocks of sphagnum moss (were they always there?), and my veins divided and opened, overflowing with blood as clear as Anya's. The tree roots entangled in my toes, I stretched and engulfed, fed and watered, laughed and nurtured. And Anya's hands caressed mine, our lips met, our hearts beat as one. I felt the leshy nearby, getting stronger, feeding on us, melding with us, mud and water, blood and moss, lichen and stone.

I did not know how many days had passed, but the trees came back to life—the spruces had regrown their needles, and the birches stood surrounding by a pale halo of young greenery. The leshy, healthy and exuberant, disengaged himself from the tree roots and my mires, and stood once again in a human form next to Anya's shore. I followed his example and deflated and creaked, putting myself back together. My skin had grown green like my hair, and mushrooms sprouted where my fingers used to be. "Turn her back," I said. I would take care of myself later.

"As you wish."

The water of the lake agitated and formed a pillar, still and shining like glass. Then its surface clouded, as if someone spilled milk into it, and Anya's sweet face looked at me without reproach. She stepped onto the shore of an empty lake basin, her skin clear, her hair long and golden, flowing down her shoulders. My breath caught in my throat, and simultaneously I grew self-conscious and ashamed. She was so pretty and perfect, and I had become a nasty, ugly thing. A swamp kikimora, fit only to frighten travelers and give children nightmares.

The leshy and Anya smiled at me, unfazed.

"I can't go back like this," I said to the leshy. "Can you make me the way I used to be?"

"If that's what you want." He shrugged with pretend indifference, and looked away.

"Anya?"

She shook her head. "I'd rather stay." Her voice lilted and sung, like a creek jumping from stone to stone. "What's back there? What do you miss?"

I stumbled for words. There was nothing there but the cold and the wolf-year, eager to tear out every jugular. Nothing but the shifty-eyed people, quickly dismantling everything that we ever knew, everything that retained a shred of meaning. Nothing but money that no one had but everyone wanted.

"Well?" the leshy said. "Should I turn you into a girl and send you on your way?" A spark danced inside his deep tree hole eyes, as if he already knew what I was going to say.

"I'm not a girl," I said. "I'm a kikimora." I wrapped one arm around Anya's soft waist, and the other around the snags of the leshy's shoulders, becoming a deep morass between a crystal clear lake and a dark forest, an in-between, a bridge between water and land, past and future, now and forever.

SONG TO THE SELKIE
GEMMA FILES

Man into seal, the legend lingers,
derived from tales told on moonlit sand.
Pain after pain, the delusion: Six fingers
cradled in a weeping mortal woman's hand.

Fur, sleek, slips through love and water
while frightened hands dance away like fish
from their demon lovers' flesh.

Each generation spawns new dreamers
willing to wait lifetimes on a broken shore
for the rising tide—ever golden-eyed—
of selkies caught in nets of lies
(human-spun) which surface once,
and then are seen no more.

The shark-teeth of desire in their skins
catch and cloy 'till, going down,
they are no longer children of two worlds. They drown.

We are too complex for these creatures
who have no ambition to walk further on the land.
Those who, without the privilege of choice,
are swept out further than a human voice
can fathom—across the depths, the empty reaches—
for reasons neither of us understand.

SILENCE, BEFORE THE HORN
MARIE BRENNAN

In the end, we all chose sleep. Skuld was the first to go; they say she went to Svalbard, to the glaciers that never melt, and locked in ice she dreams the centuries away. Thrúth sleeps in stone, Hrist in the bole of an ancient tree. Brynhild chose fire, and left it once, but to fire she returned, immolating herself to escape a greater pain.

And I? I chose water. The gentle lap of waves on a lakeshore, in a distant land where I thought I would not be disturbed. We were tired, all of us, tired of choosing the slain, tired of the endless round of battle and death. We chose instead to sleep: a little death we granted to ourselves.

But my sleep did not last. A magician, a worker of charms, divined what lay beneath the surface of my lake. He served a warrior, and brought him there, and the warrior demanded my sword from me.

And I? I gave it up. Let another choose who would die. But a valkyrie, it seems, cannot renounce her nature so easily. Had he not taken my sword, he would have lived to great age, and his shining kingdom would have endured for generations to come. As it was, he died in battle: I chose him, and he was slain.

Perhaps he wanted it that way.

When he lay dying on the shore, he returned the sword to me. Twice his companions refused, but at his word they came a third time and flung the blade over the water. I caught it as it flew, one white-clad arm rising above the surface of the lake. I wonder what his companions made of that.

He carouses now in the Allfather's hall, waiting with the others for the end that will come. Or he sleeps under a hill: a more dignified image. Either is true, or neither, or both. It does not matter. He waits, and will return.

And I? I wait as well. We cannot sleep forever. We will take our rest while we can, I in my lake, Skuld in ice, Brynhild in fire. We will rise when the horn sounds, and do battle, and die: a death chosen for us when time began.

OLD STORM SHADOW
LILA GARROTT

The white bird calling at my window
would pick berries from my mouth if I allowed her,
would crush my heart's compliance into winter,
would lock me in a tower full of princesses
unable to remember themselves, nightingales.
I've some few words for passion, or for freedom,
but she, a harp for pain, unstrings my logos.
Harpy, there's the heart of it, and all compliance
as she allows the window glass to shatter her
into a thousand pieces, all unspeakable.

Be my veil between before and afterward
and I will give you everything I've found again;
take a little leave of me and I regenerate
so you come back again, daemon of the shivering,
and harvest like the ghost of every usurer.
I cannot dance, nor seek another counselor.
We might as well admit we are inseparable:
veil me with leaf-mold and my shivered ghost
will haunt you in your other incarnations
as your pain that forces you to cry in silence.

You have no life but what my body gives you
and the bird-wings of the winter, beating, breaking.
If I make into pain the tongueless nightingale,
then I must be the swallow, laughing it:
daemon, elsewhere there is harvest for you,
elsewhere there is endless separation,
but here my window cancels your reflection;
my life bears gifts to break the beating pain again.
The sun will rise; my lips are stained with berries;
my heart, bereft of weakness, chooses struggle.

THE CLAIRVOYANT, BETWEEN DARK & DREAM

MIKE ALLEN

Impossible to sleep when your inner eyes won't close,
stare fixed and blank at the night's offerings, no matter
how filthy or banal; captive audience as strange parades
array along shifting hilltops or march through narrowing halls.

But tonight, no parades at all—nothing
but a mud-brown plain, flat to horizon and beyond,
air thick with purple and crimson, bruised meat haze,
skinned mist. Then
                — what's this?—
gunmetal grey forms stretch the membrane of sky,
force themselves out of ether, etch themselves on air,
titanic clunking gears, stratospheric chains,
shapes of drums and beams and pipes and boilers,
hungry, crawling god-machines
city-crushing spokes slicing down
wheels to grind continents like soft clay.

But in the next instant, gone, sudden as began,
leviathan outlines scattered into dust

by down-burst winds, breaths from other gods
even more depraved; the power
in their cyclone blow
stirs up the plain below, showing you
(What are you, here?

                     Remote angel observer?
Unblinking sun engaged in single focus point?)
how the plain stirs, not solid at all:
brown flakes swirling toward Heaven,
tornado-strewn leaves—

                     closer still, and you see,
not leaves at all, but skins, withered paper shells.
Kites without tethers, they fly, expanded by
the whim of gale to crude semblances of what was.
Arms flap as if seeking purchase, mouths
gape in dried ovals, heads sway on flimsy necks
as if struggling to make sense of it all.
And the faces? Far-flung strangers?

Or are they familiar,
remnants of people you know?

You are shrinking, rising, Eye in retreat,
too distant as the leaf-like things fall away;
unable to tell, as the liquid void of real sleep
pours in, Deluge of Oblivion. No way

to ever truly know: have you glimpsed
the fate of all Fate,
                      or merely your own?

LITTLE MATCH GIRL
YOON HA LEE

matchstick caress
of light upon light
on your lips

a feast of candied fire
candled color
heat that haunts

a match's kiss dies
in smoke and promises
one more, one taste

another test of your
starveling touch
before winter wins

THE LASS OF LOCH ROYAL
HOLLY PHILLIPS

"Who will shoe my pretty little foot?
Who will glove my hand?
And who will kiss my ruby lips
When you're in a foreign land?"

"Your papa will shoe your pretty little foot,
Your mama can glove your hand,
And I will kiss your ruby lips
When I return again."

*

A cut flower, her sisters call him, mortal and sweet in his dying. He fills their father's house with his fragrance, his presence ephemeral, thinning into the air. He says he is dreaming. Says she is a dream, and touches her to make her real. She touches him. Solid with flesh and bone, rough with hair, warm and smelling of animal musks and sea-salt sweat, blood, tears: *ghost*, she thinks, holding him, watching him drift away from her into time.

Her sisters laugh at her in their cold garden. Her father, rich and careless with experience, lets her go her own way.

She takes her lover to a chamber her father has half forgotten. Marble and plaster slump and twist like candle wax, like tree roots and water-shaped stone. The carpet is mossy, emerald green welling up out of the pattern of blue and red and gold; the bed curtains hang in leafy tatters; the wine is pale amber, bright as honey, as water from a sunlit forest stream. She watches her lover's eyes, and sees him see a dream.

He is dark-eyed, like a stag, his hair like glossy chestnuts, his neck powerful as if with the weight of antlers or horns. He moves through his dreams like a deer through the woods, alert, wary, proud. She draws his hands to her fine skin, her breasts, the slight curve of her belly. He is incandescent with desire, with life, so brilliant, delicate, fleeting. He says he loves her, but what does he love? What does he touch? What does he see?

He slips away, away, away into dreams. If he stays, her father tells her, he will soon be gone for good.

*

> "Now if I had a sailing boat
> And a man to sail with me,
> I'd sail tonight to my own lad
> If he will not come to me."

> Her father gave her a sailing boat,
> He sent her to the strand.
> She took her baby in her arms
> And turned her back on the land.

*

She has been anchored to the floor of time. The true world, her father's world, slips about her, beneath her, as uneasy as her lover's sleep, as uneasy as the rolling sea. She has become tangled in her lover's dream, and discovers—the first fear of her life—that she does not know if he still dreams of her. What will she be if he forgets?

The ocean smells of him, of life and death commingled.

The ship, built of trees from her father's wood, sings to her with her sisters' voices. The silent boatman listens. Conducting his choir of sails and ropes, winds and waves, he gives her nothing but the music of their passage. Even he has become vague to her. With the child weighing like a stone in her arms, she is being dragged through layers of time into the cold and mortal depths. She lays her cheek against the child's sleeping head. He smells of roses and alder leaves. He smells of the sea.

*

She was not a-sailing about three months,
It was not more than four,
When there she rode her sailing boat
Up to her lover's door.

She took her baby in her arms
And to his door she's gone.
She's knocked and cried and knocked again
But answer got she none.

*

The sand is cold beneath her feet and sharp with shells. Her father's boatman will wait, but when she looks back, across the creaming swirl of the broken waves, she is bewildered. Is that her father's boat there, with its singing masts and sails of living green? It is as if she sees two worlds. In her left eye, her father's ship, a gentle breeze playing upon the harp of the shrouds. In her right eye, a fisherman's dory, its oars propped against the stern, its gunwales painted green. She blinks. It is cold dawn. There is mist curling above the foam. She turns and begins to walk, barefoot and balancing between her father's world and time.

The child, rousing from his sleep, reaches with both hands, she does not know for which.

A world in either eye. Sand reaches up to pebbles, pebbles give way to rounded stones dark with damp from the fog.

Above the stones rise tumbled logs bleached the color of whale bones, a low cliff divided by streams and waves and noisy with waking gulls. Above the stones rises a bleached boardwalk mended with iron nails, crooked houses with gleaming slate roofs, their painted shutters closed like doors between the chill of morning and the stirring of human life. In both worlds, the stones are icy beneath her feet. She thinks of her sisters' garden, and suffers a moment of confusion. Where is she? Why is she here?

Then she remembers her lover's startled, wondering eyes, and understands something about him she had not quite grasped before. She hopes he still loves her. She hopes he will take the child into his world and let her return to hers.

She walks into the human town.

*

> "Open the door my own true love,
> Open the door I pray,
> For your young child that's in my arms
> Will be dead before it is day."

> "Go away you wild woman,
> Here you won't get in.
> Go drown you in the salt, salt sea
> Or hang on the gallows pin."

*

Dame Johanna sleeps in her chair before the fire these days, guarding the stairs to the chambers above. She does not fear that her son will rise from his bed and creep away with the night. He sleeps the way other sons drink or gamble or whore, breaking their mothers' hearts. Dame Johanna could almost wish he would go out to the taverns, if only he would come home again rough-voiced and staggering, reeking of beer and cheap perfume, and not with haunted eyes and a face so worn with longing he seems a stranger, a man who has suffered some terrible thing, not her own laughing boy. Not her own laughing boy.

Dame Johanna sits before the guttering fire, her feet wrapped in a sheep's skin, hearing the big house lean and stretch as the servants wake and begin to stir. Soon the groom will come in from the stable with the first armload of wood. Soon the cook will stump sleepily down the stairs to wake the kitchen fire. Soon Dame Johanna will rise and stretch like an aging cat, aching and sharp-clawed with fatigue, and go upstairs to call her son, stroke his hair and shake his arm and shout his name, if need be, so he will wake and stare at her with those dark, red-rimmed, stranger's eyes, and swear that today he will get up. Today he will eat. Today he will be well.

Soon.

*

"Don't you mind, my true love,
When we were at the wine,
We changed our rings on our fingers
And the best of them was mine.

And don't you mind, my true love
The vows you made to me.
We swore an oath between us both
For the years that are to be."

*

He pours himself into sleep like a pitcher of water into a well. Awake, he is an exile, cast out of paradise, his own promise a worthless key, for he cannot find the door. Waking, he cannot believe the door exists. Sleeping, he remembers, he hopes, he courts his dreams.

He lies like a child with his hand curled beneath his cheek. Her ring is too small to wear; he clasps it between fingers and palm, always cold, never warming to his mortal flesh. *She* warmed to him. Aching, denied release, he stirs between his sheets. Desire feeds on him like a fever. He feeds on desire, a starving man, a thirsty man drowning in a well. (He stirs, turns, clenches his arms across his chest. He holds sleep fast, he will not let it go.)

He dreams of doors. Always, always, he dreams of doors. The deep shadowed promise of them. The mystery of even the humblest portal. He walks barefoot through his town, trying the latches of the baker's shop, the chandler's, the house of the girl he loved when he was twelve. The doors swing open, stand ajar on nothing, on board floors and coarse tables and human shadows who turn and stare, seeing nothing. He is not there, a phantom at the threshold they cannot see. He stands at his own door, a ghost in his own life, and turns away without knocking, afraid. The town is gone. There are boulders cleft by trees, white roots snaking through dark rock, moss and ferns, a spring that seeps through grass as long and fine as a woman's hair. He is thirsty in his dream, kneels and drinks. He hears knocking, voices, a wind like a keening song (he curls around his sleep, clutching it with all his limbs, her fisted ring to his mouth) and knows in the way of dreaming that he is inside, that when he turned from his door he stepped inside his true life at last, and she is outside, begging to be let in. The tables turned. In the dream, he is alight with joy. His desire lends him its fever strength. But when he stands and looks around, he is still in the stony wood, and still, still, he cannot find the door to let her in.

*

> "Go away you wild woman,
> Here you won't get in!
> Go drown you in the salt, salt sea
> Or hang on the gallows pin!"

> Day did dawn and the cock did crow
> And the sun begin to peep
> When there he rose, her own true love,
> And sorely he did weep.

*

The question that would haunt Dame Johanna, the question she never asked herself, a ghost question like the ghost of an unborn child, was this:

Why, when she hated his sleep so terribly—when she hated it like an enemy, like his murderer, like death—why, when she hated his sleep, did she protect it as if she were protecting her son? Why did she shield his dreams?

Why did she refuse to let him be awakened?

The question Dame Johanna never asked. That does not mean it has no answer.

*

> "Mother, I dreamed of my true love,
> She lives across the sea.
> I dreamed she'd come to my front door,
> A-weeping sore for me."
>
> "There was a lady here last night
> With a baby in her arms,

But I would not let her in to you
For fear she'd do you harm."

*

The child was heavy. He weighed in her arms like an anchor stone, his swaddling wet, his cold fists tangled in her hair. Seagulls cried his hunger for him. He was silent, puzzled, his dark gaze upon his mother's face. She saw herself in his eyes, her cheeks wet with human tears. Herself in both the child's eyes. The child in both of hers. Which world was she seeing when she looked at him? Which world did he see when he looked at her? The child. Her child. Her dreaming lover's son.

The foam coiled soft and cold around her calves. The sea turned like a restless sleeper against the sand. Her father's ship slipped in to shore, the water of two seas bearing the great hull close to the land. She felt the shadow of her father's boatman cool the air about her, cloaking the sea-smell in lightning, oak leaves, and wind. She did not so much as glance at him, afraid to look away from herself in her child's eyes. She handed the child to the boatman, and pulled herself aboard, never looking away. Never looking away. Her child watched her, holding her fast, and even so, for an instant she dimmed in the dark mirror of his gaze. For an instant, she felt rough wood beneath her hands, the startled shift and weave of a tiny boat upon the surf. But the boatman lent her his hand, and then she had the child in her arms again. She clutched him against the terrified beating of her heart.

Her father had warned her how easily her lover might have been lost in his dreams, in their world. He had never told her how easy it would be for her to lose herself in her lover's place.

*

>He ran, he ran to the salt sea shore,
>He looked out on the foam,
>When there he spied his true love's boat
>A-tossing toward her home.
>
>He called, he cried, he waved his hands,
>He begged her sore to stay,
>But the more he called and the more he cried
>The louder roared the sea.

*

She felt safer with the child in her arms. Lulled by the ship's song, he dozed, his head pillowed on her shoulder, her hair still tangled in his chubby hands. She buried her face in the warm angle of his neck, breathing his scent, alder-rose, so much like her own, tainted only a little by the salt, salt sea. Sometimes the ship's song was drowned by the clamor of the gulls. Sometimes the steady deck dipped and slid beneath her feet, uncertain as the waves. But she held on to her son, onto her life, onto her world. She held on.

Until, over the sound of the gulls, the waves, the ship's song, she heard her lover's voice.

*

> Now the wind did blow and the sea rose up,
> It tossed her boat on shore.
> It laid his true love at his feet,
> But he saw his son no more.
>
> The first he kissed her ruddy cheeks,
> The next he kissed her chin,
> And the last he kissed her ruby lips:
> There was no breath within.

*

He touched her with a kind of joy. She was real, she was true, she was his to hold once more against his heart. She had found the door he could not have found in all a lifetime of dreams. She would show him the way through to his true life. She would take him home.

*

"O woe be to you, ill mother,
And an ill death may you die!
You have not been the death of one,
You've been the death of three!"

With thanks to Paddy Tutty, who collected "The Lass of Loch Royal" and recorded it on The Roving Jewel.

LAMENT FOR ALEXANDER
SHIRL SAZYNSKI

Son of the Sun, the shadow of Dionysos hangs over you:

What dark hand dried your bright tears?
No woman's, nor eunuch—
your father's hand, rough-made for war?
    So you conquered.
You understood:
a strength that breaks is useless—
and tamed a fractious spirit by your hands' insistence
gentle, though trained to kill.

So your first victory remained, ever at your side
bearing you to war.
A horse for whom
entire tribes were slain,
in ransom.
Scorched by the heat of your own glory,
did you seek release?

Did they fight within you, brother-Gods?
Did he creep upon you,

forgotten god of war?
—or did you seek him out
in those last, bright lonely days

a salve against betrayal?

HELEN
JOSELLE VANDERHOOFT

Look closely: here is a thing mounted
beneath bulletproof glass
like a flight of butterflies stopped short with silver pins.
See, she stands
between *Les Demoiselles D'Avignon* and the *Virgin of the Rocks*.
The face that launched a thousand ships preserved
by mummy engines and formaldehyde tears,
too much charcoal ringing her blue eyes
open to the world like her sex
which small men fear and poets praise—
Eva Peron in an attic dress.

Look closely,
and do not listen . . .

She is our main attraction, finer perhaps,
than anything in God's Genesis Period
(Eve and bat-winged Lillith, suffering Sarai)
because she, she—
Look closely, now! Her nipples sprout red ink and her tongue

drips fly paper delectable to men
and women.
Despite the glass
the watch dogs
the iron grates dropped nightly on this gallery,
sometimes burglars of both sexes enter through the ceiling
and write doggerel verses on her skin,
odes to a Greecian, spurned.
We keep them locked with her, as memories.
Graffiti, after all, is the finest form of social commentary.

The echoes in this room are fierce.
Hear them hiding behind
an amphora, a quilted tapestry,
a goddess made of snakes.
The sneak along the floor, creep up your spine
and dash into your brains a soporific SOS.
Most of all beware the echoes of this docent's voice
They would devour you.

He says, he says,
she was and is a slut,
a luxurious divan wrapped in silk and pearls
upon which Paris lay and spent himself.
Lusty cunt, she got what she deserved;
a head shaved and Menelaus proud

as the Trojan women looked on and laughed
behind white-knuckled hands smeared
with dirt and rain.

She says, she says,
she is not your blackboard
Or your pissing contest. She was a rope for two
bull-horned men, who could not see the forest
for the trees, or her for her breasts and lovely hair
so they, they they,
they tore her in two and left her
vivisected like Rembrant's corpse,
the anatomy of a rape for posterity
to dissect with laughing scalpels
(exhibition of *Your Gaze Hits the Side of My Face*
to follow shortly).

Look closely,
But don't listen . . .

They say and say
mouths feasting at her tits like Errour's books
that she's Duessa, the virginslut
raised up on a mountain of sighs and implications
while all the while the tourists snap their photographs
here just to see the Mona Lisa smile

but happy, nonetheless, for this five-act play
of ink and flesh.

But look now,
Look.
This is the best part, see
the reason why everyone
Americans to Zelanders
pay such a steep price for admission.
See!
There's something in the fluid that we used
to fill her veins and stop her bird-like heart
(so pretty in our palms when we removed it)
If you look closely see, her
See
See
See

She
She
She

It looks like she is crying. And everyone
the men and women and the tourists all —
some say and some do not, but it's all true.
They like it when she cries.

She has a face that launched a thousand ships
and yet it also smiled its way
around a chocolate popsicle. She laughed once
at the sight of butterflies, when one
with its brown-honey wings
perched on her tremulous wrist. She read Shakespeare,
but if you asked her, candidly, she preferred Milton.
She liked knitting
Just as much as she liked hiking in the rain,
And devising engines for a steam powered ship
To bring her father home.

She played kick ball
(badly) and soccer (better). She dreamed of writing books
when it was cold outside.
She got lonely,
and sometimes she felt fat.

But, it didn't matter, after her Fall
through glass and nails,
and goddesses with teeth
that raked like heroine lines.
Then there was only Paris
Meneleus
Helen

And the stringy sex that bound them up
In a toxic candy apple wrapped in gold foil.

That's why, that's why . . .

That isn't why she's here!

Pay no attention to those Demoiselles!
That rocky Dame, the smiling Signora!
Paintings lie, you see. And they have drapes.
We'll draw them now,
protect them from the air and from the rot
that creeps on painted ladies' foreheads.
I think they're jealous; their masters lacked the spark
This Helen-thing possesses. So
they make up stories
About echoes
Candy apples
Devouring things!
They make no sense.
They are, I think, ridiculous.

Come closer now and see
see, see
Her skin's as thin as a Baedeker's Guide
from 1893.

Come closer, closer
See,
She's waiting.
Why don't you dip a pen
in her red ink
and write a message to her
on her face?

I know the regulations,
That I'm not supposed to
open the case unless for VIPs.
But you,
You
You
You're so very, very
Important.
We want to know your feelings
on this woman-work.
So, leave a message scrawled
across her breasts
her thighs
her ageless hips
made smooth with mummy
Tell her
Tell her
Your 3 a.m. thoughts

Your bottled confessions
The princes in your attic
Your adulterous transgressions.
The spleen you cannot say unless
you say it in your dreams

Come closer,
Closer
Your footsteps and your pens
echo in the chambers of her heart
like bullets, but she only smiles
and cries
a little doll who
knows
who knows,
who knows . . .

Look closely
And listen. Please.
I was a woman, once.

NYMPHS FINDING THE HEAD OF ORPHEUS
THEODORA GOSS

The water has a dim and glassy hue.
A mass of airy bubbles clings to curls
That tumble through the river-bottom's marls,
And cypresses hang heavy with their woe.

Our hair-tips touch the water's urgent tow
As we lift this possessor of blue lips
And single eye that out its substance weeps
From the dark river bound by thorny may.

Now sing, my sisters, piercingly and slow,
And sweetly as the honey of the comb,
For this rank weed, and beat the hollow drum,
And kiss and turn the leperous cheeks away.

REVULSION AND THE BEAST
VERA NAZARIAN

You chose beauty over truth, my beloved. And beauty chose you.

Beauty is wise.

She had seen all the way down to your innards past the mangled coarse fur and the crumpled boar-skin, past the eyes of hell and the maw of midnight . . .

She had seen down, deeper yet, to the level of smallest things, where boundaries break down and the edge of a knife blade is a wide plateau, where dust motes are suns and the nigh-invisible thing that makes up who we are is connected to all else—that is how far down she looked. There, at last, among the infinite worlds nestled within the span of a teardrop's membrane, was your single point of light.

And she latched onto it.

Beauty is relentless; she pulled you forth.

Later, in your accursed castle, the two of you played the game of stripping outer layers and the shedding of skins—nothing more, really, than a lovers' tension-dance. You tried to open her, grant you that much, but all you had was her radiant surface. And since there is nothing more impenetrable than such homogeneity, you were convinced that she was thus throughout. She, on the other hand, peeled you layer by layer in her mind, ever clasping your point of light, until she saw the beast facade crumble, and underneath a simple wounded thing—a human thing.

Beauty is wise and relentless.

I watched you as you returned triumphant to our father's house, how you proclaimed her as your wife and lover, and the mother of your children unto the ages. From my recessed window in the attic, I drank in the sight of your previously grotesque form now transformed into a similar keen beauty as hers. You were sleek and perfect like my sister, but more angular, as befits a man. I longed to put my fingers to the electric surface of your blond hair. Just to feel a shock . . .

At last, you were a true man in their eyes. My father, the old bourgeoisie of the town, the righteous circumspect clergy, all accepted you, since now they could be certain of the fine, stiff velvet of your doublet overlying a man's body. Though, despite what you may think, and no matter their initial indignation, they had accepted you even earlier—not admitting to themselves even, that in the world property is sufficient proof of humanity.

With them it was instinctual as soon as father had returned bearing twenty oak chests filled with old doubloons and faded ancient lace encrusted with pearls and faceted topaz. They had accepted you with the sensual need that this town has for gold and old nobility, even though you were the Beast.

And protest as loudly as they might, they would have had you ravish my sister in your old horrifying form, without a blink, if you had also borne the title of Prince, or if a drop of regal blood diluted the ebony ichor in your beastly veins.

Only, we had seen you as a man long before all of this even began. We, daughters of this house.

When you cast your lure of seeking and glanced into the scrying mirror, looking for your fair redeemer, we also could see in our ordinary mirrors the reflected shadow of your burning hell-gaze. Bonds had been established even then.

We felt you in our guts—nay, in our wombs—my sisters and I. And she, the Beauty, she felt you in her pupils. For a fortnight your burning hell glanced out at us from all reflecting surfaces in our house, and riddled our nightmares. Tormented, we walked at all times with lit candles. And because of your intrusion, we in turn glanced into each other's souls. Thus, when you chose her with a single impulse of need, we all knew the moment.

There was one other moment of significance, when in passing you had seen me, and you had recoiled, as in all fairness you must. For I am thus, not to be borne, even at the level of my soul. I am called Revulsion.

You had seen me and recoiled, you who were the Beast. I was exactly like you, but deeper than the skin. For the part of you that was the quagmire on the outside was what filled me throughout. I was dark all the way *in*.

And in my homogeneity, I frightened you.

My sister, who is both Beauty and Wisdom, is the only one who had never feared me, the only one who could see the nature of my darkness. Beauty would come to me and sit in my monk-like cell, as I reposed against the grand faded pillows of soft antique linen, my form shrunken with muscular atrophy. We would remain thus in silence, while the sun traversed the haze of sky outside the small window, past the curling vines of ivy.

We sat listening to the calls of birds outside, and the rush of the wind as it moved past the towering walls of our ancient house. I saw the meandering lines of rivers in the distance, and the faraway lumps of shadow that were the mountains. I saw the roads and the rooftops of the closest houses, and the single needle spire of the cathedral, piercing the sky.

They say that the needles of the church-spires are sharp, so that they could pierce heaven and prick the soul of God, so that He would remember us, hear our cries, and look down.

I spent long hours calling Him with my mind. Calling, so that He would take me away.

But the only one who ever heard or remembered me was my sister, Beauty and Wisdom.

I call her Wisdom even now. That is my own singular name for her, for while beauty fades, wisdom remains everlasting.

Wisdom sat by my side, and took me by my clammy misshapen hand. And sometimes she would tell me rambling tales of distant wonder, in a breathy childish voice that had imprinted upon me so well.

Her voice dispelled, for a moment, my dark. And when she, my only visitor, would depart, leaving me to my self, I remembered again what I was, remembered and allowed the thick stagnant waters of self-revulsion to rush back, to cover me. And in the twilight, in the long hours of night, before I ravaged sleep—for sleep, too, would refuse to come to me voluntarily, so that I had to hunt down and plunder *it* for a taste of gentle oblivion—I burned with the emptiness, the ugly filthy hatred of the self.

And sometimes, in flashes, I remembered you, my beloved.

You are never mine; I know it well. But allow me this false sweetness for a moment, if only in my mind. Thus, my beloved.

Ever since the first time you insinuated into our souls, looking for her, there was a link established. I know not whether my other sisters felt it as strongly as I did, for they, not unlike Beauty, had real existences, while I spent every moment here, decaying. It is no wonder that their momentary awareness of you would be eclipsed with the richness of their own private moments, the moments of their daily lives. The reflecting surfaces, the mirrors of our house revealing glimpses of hell shadows, were all quickly forgotten.

I, on the other hand, lived vicariously through all of them, and most of all through you and Beauty. At odd hours of the night I would be disturbed by pricklings of intensity, by touches of your mind and hers, as you loved each other in the tumult of darkness. In the cool mornings, when lilac haze stands upon the world outside and the sun is still swaddled in yesterday, I felt touches of crisp air upon your cheeks as you walked the gardens of our father's house. And at high noon, when warm heady scents arise from the distant harvest land, I could feel the coolness of your hand in hers as you shared a repast of mead and freshly baked bread. Each sweet, rich, fierce burst of flavor, each bite, was mine also; still is.

I suppose this link will always be there, until my own life ebbs away. And while I feel the moments of your life, can you feel me also? I hope with all my dark heart that you do not.

This mirror must reflect one way only.

Do not feel or hear me, my beloved. My intrusion upon your light would stain you, would sully you and my sister Wisdom.

Only once had my intrusion served well. That one time, I know it had, for I had cried out to both of you, and it came from my deepest hidden wilderness, the profound true voice of my being.

It was when you lay dying, still locked in your Beast form, on the grounds of your fearsome castle in the deepening twilight. My sister had broken her promise to return to you, had forgotten you in the familiar joys of living in our father's house. Your pain was so acute that it had reached out to me, and rebounded through me like a sympathetic string. I rang with pain, tolled with it, played it. I was pain; hence, I was you.

In my tiny cell, I had cried out, and my voice was but a whisper, yet it reverberated through my mind like the bells of all the cathedrals put together.

And Beauty heard me.

She heard my pitiful cry, the cry of sister Revulsion, and she remembered. And through me she saw you.

Only for a moment, I was your divine link.

But that moment was enough. What ensued next is known to everyone, and the result is blessed history.

I am glad to have served you well that once. Maybe it is the reason I was put on this earth, the reason to justify this creature that is myself, this Revulsion?

But, no matter. You chose well, my beloved, by choosing beauty over truth.

For truth is, Beauty loves you from her heights, while I love you from the bowels of hell which is all the same throughout, all *me*, and my need for you is dark like my homogenous being. There would be no relief, and I would pull you back down with me into the beastly abyss.

Beauty is wise, but Revulsion is a madwoman.

BASKETS FULL OF GODS
RIO LE MOIGNAN

A thin figure sits at the crossroads,
wound in colourless cloth and tiny bells:
they chime in the breeze, but toll like temple gongs
when he moves to greet travellers.
Wide baskets, woven from wool and willow and bones,
wait in the warm flecked shade
cast by an olive sapling.

The artificer-priest waits for those in need.
His baskets are full of hopes,
gods-in-potentia,
motley shells and frames to be filled or clothed,
and infused with belief.
He exchanges them for food,
or promises of shelter,
medicines and blankets and songs:
things that were made by hands and heart,
as he made their dreams.
Songs and food for himself,
and gifts for the sick and for times of trouble.

The puppet-forms wait in the silvergreen light
filtered down through the leaves.
Deities are bartered, not bought or given for nothing,
but there are few rituals or reasons,
all else is mutable, personal, chosen.
People get the gods they can believe in,
the divinity they wish for.
The gods they hold within are released by belief,
and housed in mirrors and dolls and shrines.

They slumber in their wicker beds, not yet numinous,
not until they are taken home and told what they are:
named, or painted, or simply set in their place.
Decorated with ribbons, perhaps, or kissed
or offered flowers and fruit,
sand, blood, conversation or salt.
Cage-sculptures are filled with a bird,
metal bowls may hold wood-shavings or incense, and fire.
Then they live. Some give out light
while others speak in riddles; a few merely watch.

Babies are given cloth godlets,
soft, portable; protector-playmates.
Others must pick their own:
seek out a muse or numen or totem;
select safety or meaning from amongst empty shells.

A god for a birthday, a journey—for change.
One god or many, to worship or fear or forget.

People make gods, but who can read their own soul?
Few awake the gods they expect.

IN THE NAME OF . . .
ANNA TAMBOUR

What god gives men blank checks
to spend life liquidly in his name?
The same that sits calmly
watching almond trees
explode pink blossoms
into smoky skies
to snow upon
the rubbled flesh
of others of his
created.

What god
celebrates
his name being called
as the last act before murder—
the Act of our species.
We have created
the creature called War—
with a longer memory
than the elephant
and a longer tail

to lash the living
throughout the
generations.

What god pets this creature,
warms to its purr?
No god, for we were made—
our species—not for hating,
but to mate together.

God's-will,
we should be making mongrels now,
not war.

MOTHER IS A MACHINE
CATHERYNE M. VALENTE

They gnash from the door, the slavering parent-golems, offering wire hangers and arsenic cakes with grimy grins, teeth sliding in their heads, grunting their nicotine-paean in 4/4 time.

They lurch and leer, sewing their fingertips to my mouth—
Hush, child, hush.

There are windows in their bellies, and in them I can see homunculi vomiting earthly delights onto the titanium floor. In them I can see the quantum zygote, the almost-me, the tiny machines that might have been daughters echoing in and out of each other with quiet, regular clicks.

Clockwork girl, shine and smile, polish the apples of your cheeks, we've company tonight.

Mother is a machine. Father is a factory. He stamps out hundreds of tiny fathers a day from his bronze-age femur, two by two by two. Her tin breasts are bolted to a steel-drum chest; his hydraulic arms pump up and down on my rot-soft stomach, cut biscuit-daughters from my liver, from my kidneys: little pig-tailed pancreatic automata that scowl and weep and scowl and weep. And on nights when the moon is fat and yeasty as unbaked bread, Mother opens her ribs and tells me, tells me, with her mouth flapping open like a swinging door, to crawl inside, baby girl, crawl crawl crawl. Her wheedle-voice hisses, steam-sighing, from a copper jaw, hinged with a platinum pin.

See, saw, Margaery Daw, sold her bed and lay upon straw!

She beckons into herself with eight-jointed hands. I am afraid to be inside Mother, whose window looks in but never out;

I am afraid to be inside Mother, whose ribs are made from beaten spoons and the spittle of Spanish silversmiths;

I am afraid to be inside Mother, whose doors slam hungry and grim. Her kettle-cry reverberates and conjugates the nursery-verb into she and I, she and I:

Oh! One misty, moisty morning, when cloudy was the weather! There I met an old man, clothed all in leather!

Father bangs on the womb-dead-door and she eats his electroplated thumb-knuckles with slurping candy-smiles—I touch the back of her breasts and try to hear a code tapped out, a code mapped out on her steely lungs.

Cilia, cilia, all this delicate lace! Mother is a machine, and I am empty space.

I am wire, ash, and never a beanstalk floating out of my throat, sliding up to the Father-press, sliding up to the warehouse window. Mother pats her belly, full and warm. Mother slaps her chest-door shut and dances her banshee-shuffle, crouched and laughing.

The cat's in the cupboard and she can't see!

Here they come and here they are, the parent-golems with their eyes in their hair, and when I am let out, when I am let out of the steel-drum torso, the metal tans my skin gill-gray.

Ask me, Father, ask me which biscuit-girl I will have for breakfast, which of my selves I shall eat while you chortle above my pretty sea-snail scalp and sew my skin to a stucco wall—which shall I have, the I that dresses for Christmas in syringes and horse-hoof-glue, the I that slavers just like you?

Ask me, Mother, ask me if I thirst to breathe the fluid of your cylinder-self, ask me if I leap to be closed in, folded in, tucked into you? *Now I lay me down to sleep inside your engine-bones. And should I die before I wake, the clocks will eat their own.*

Ask me when you hem my hips, ask me when you thread my nose, ask me when you solder pilgrim's palm to pilgrim's palm, ask me when you hide me in your silver bowels if I would not rather have my own hands to eat?

I see the moon, the moon sees me, bright as only the moon can be!

Father is a factory. Mother is a machine. Father presses out my skin like a book—fifth edition, Coptic binding; out of his mouth drops copy, copy, copy. Mother pulls me back in until there is only one of her, and I am under the larynx, stitching the old electric umbilicus together with glabrous teeth.

Stitch it up, and stitch it down, then I'll give you half a crown!

Push it in, Father, all this metal! Make it mine, my pure mercury, pour it cool and trickling into my marrow and I will wake up strong and shining, I will wake up new. Into your belly, Mother, in I go, and if there is enough wire and lead, I can make a merrily clanging creature, I can build a child like you.

Mother is copper, Father is tin.
But I am bone, but I am skin.

INSIDE THE TOWER
STEPHANIE BURGIS

Light streams into the single tower room, onto the bed. Too much light, too bright, too harsh. I don't want to see my mother's emaciated face so clearly; I can't bear to see the hollows that formed in her cheeks while I was gone, or her dark eyes, staring at me with such fierce longing.

I've hated my mother for half my life, but watching her die is killing me. I stand up and hurry to the window, nearly running to grab the heavy curtains. Outside, warm sunlight streams down onto the forest below us. This was my only view for years, my only outlook onto the world. Beyond the trees, the bright pennants atop the castle flap, blown by a summer breeze. The depth of my bitterness takes me by surprise when I see them.

My life is good, now. I have to remind myself of that, my hands white-knuckled around the curtains. I can't see my cottage from here; it feels like a dream from which I've too-suddenly awoken, not the reality to which I'll soon return. Back home, my husband and our children are waiting. They're eating vegetables fresh from our garden, and the youngest children are playing with the dogs all day long, then snuggling up with them on the hearth as if they're puppies themselves. Whenever I see them like that, so tender and helpless, I feel as if my heart might break from wonder, fear, and envy. I've never experienced that freedom, that trust.

"Leave the windows open," Mother says. Her voice is cracked and weak, nothing like the harsh commanding tone I used to hear. "I need to feel the fresh air."

"Yes, Mother." I step back obediently, clenching my fists, and look away from the blue sky.

Life is carrying on outside, but here I am, back in my tower again, with the person who kept me imprisoned until I was nineteen years old.

At least she's coherent, now. When I first arrived, she was babbling, lost in the middle of one of her old hate-filled rants. I almost turned and ran.

"I remember," my mother says dreamily. "When you were a little girl, I used to braid your hair for hours. It was so soft. Like golden silk in my fingers."

I have to hold myself back from reaching up to feel my short, cropped hair. I never let it grow long anymore. "Can I make you anything to drink?" I ask. "One of your potions? If you tell me which herbs to mix—"

"No," she says. "No, I'm fine, now that you're back. Come, sit down."

She pats the mattress beside her with a blue-veined hand. Her knuckles have swollen into rocks.

Fighting all my instincts, I sit.

"We did everything together," she says. "The only person you ever wanted was me."

My mother is dying. I tell myself that. I use it to hold back the rage that wants to spill. The words of poison that want to pour out of my mouth and beat at her ravaged face the way she beat me with her fists, the first time I ever tried to find love away from her.

My prince is long-married to a suitably highborn bride. If I had known anything of the world, I would never have believed his promises.

But how could I possibly have known?

"You never even let me see anybody else," I whisper.

She blinks and pats my hand. "I kept you safe," she says. "You didn't understand. I wouldn't let anybody get close enough to hurt you."

You would never let me breathe.

I bite my lip so hard that I taste blood. "Maybe you should get some sleep," I say. "I'll work in the garden for a bit, cook us some dinner—"

"Everything outside is so dangerous," she says. Her eyes have gone unfocused; they move back and forth, searching—for what? "People everywhere. Waiting. Waiting to rob you. Hurt you. Take you away."

"Mother." I swallow. "I think you're getting too excited. Why don't you just close your eyes?"

But she doesn't seem to even hear me. "He said he would do it."

She's shivering, even though the air is warm. I reach over and pull the covers up around her. She tries to grab my hand. I pull it back.

"Who said?"

"My prince—"

"My prince!" Suddenly I'm breathing hard. I'm seventeen again, suffering the lash of her voice, her blows. "That was me, remember? My life, not yours!"

"They burned the house down," she says. "My mother, screaming. The prince and his men. They laughed. And then he looked at me."

Tears stand in her pale blue eyes, trickle down her cheeks. Nausea twists my stomach.

"You're upset," I say. "We'll talk about this later, when you're feeling better. I'll—"

"It hurt," she says, and it turns into a moan. "It hurt so much!"

"Mother—"

"And he said, if I whelped—"

"Mother, please—"

"I ran," she whispers. "I ran and ran. To a different kingdom, where he would never find me. And I built the tallest tower, to keep my baby safe. So no one could ever take her away. No one will ever hurt her. Ever."

Tears burn behind my eyes. She's gasping for breath as she talks.

"Shh," I whisper. "Please, Mother."

"But she's gone," Mother says. Her voice rises. It spirals into panic. "He took her! He hurt her! Where's she gone?" Her head jerks back; she twists it around on the pillow, eyes wild. "Where is she? Where's my daughter? Tell me! Where's my daughter? I need my daughter!"

"I'm here," I whisper. My chest is so tightly constricted, it feels like it's about to break apart.

"Stop lying to me!" she screams. "Where's my daughter?"

"It's all right." I force out the words through a throat clenched tight and burning. I reach out, through the memories. I reach through the beatings, through the suffocation and the mania. I make myself reach toward the girl who was hurt so badly, the girl who let fear warp the shape of her life.

I reach out and take her shaking hands, and I fold them between both of mine. "It's all right now, Mother," I whisper, and I watch her face tremble with longing. I look at the old woman I've been afraid of for so long. "See?" I whisper. In the distance, in the future, my husband and children are waiting for me. I'm not imprisoned. Not anymore. "I'm right here. With you."

BLACK DOG TIMES
JANE YOLEN

The world will end when the old woman
finishes her porcupine quill blanket,
though her black dog unpicks it whenever her
back is turned—Lakota legend

What can you do in these black dog times?
When the world is close to done,
And only the dog's teeth stand between us
And the ending? What can you do?
Choose to be born, stand up, pick the quills,
See through the mist, through the dark.
Sew yourself a robe, not a shroud.
Age gracefully. Take your medicine.
Have a colonoscopy. Do not complain.
Pick up your skirts, bend your aching knees,
And dance.

HOW TO BRING SOMEONE BACK FROM THE DEAD
VERONICA SCHANOES

1. Pain

It hurts to come back from the dead. And it hurts to bring someone back from the dead.

2. The Journey

There is always a journey and it is often long. You will have to take the path of pins and the path of needles. You will walk on the pins and your feet will bleed. You will walk on the needles and your feet will bleed, red like your jacket (You must always wear bright colors when you go to the underworld). This is your body mourning. It hurts to bring someone back from the dead.

You will need to be brave and to go into the woods. It is dark and cold, close and damp. You will be there for a long time. You will be on foot. By the time you come out, flashing lights and bright colors will confuse you. You will not be able to respond to them. Your open eyes will not focus, and you will not remember how to turn your head. You will long for the woods and you will not understand how to leave, how to be in the world outside of the woods. The woods will be the only real place. That is why you must bring bright colors with you-dressing all in black is a mistake. You will carry a torch in each hand as you search. Your feet will bleed. If the dead drink the blood, they will be able to speak to you, but they will not come back with you. Be careful. Do not let the person you want to bring back drink your blood.

You will travel for a long time, holding your two torches. You must not stray from the path and you must not pick the flowers. You may ask for help. You will ask the sun for direction and you will ask the moon. Neither will help you; the moon is not able and the sun is not willing. Triple Hecate will have heard screaming and she will tell you where. You may ask an old woman who sits by the path mumbling to herself. If you walk by without a word she will reveal herself to be a witch and eat you in two bites, but if you ask her for help and offer to share an apple with her, she will give you guidance. Do not throw stones at ravens. You may ask wolves for help, but you should not believe what they tell you. They do not think carefully. They do not think as we do.

You will travel a long ways in the dark. Perhaps you will have to make your way through thorns and brambles. The thorns will rip your skin and lay the delicate, palpating network of your veins exposed to the cold wind. You may be caught and the thorns will reach over to block out the sky. All you will be able to see will be the walls of thorns and you will forget that you even knew anything else. The world will become patterns of thorns, patterns whose repetitions you'd counted and memorized years ago, and never thought you'd have to see again. You will not want to leave; nothing outside of the thorns will seem real. Perhaps the thorns will take out your eyes and you will not see anything at all.

You will eat roots. Eventually you will eat stones.

3. Journey's End

You will finally find your beloved. She will be chained in outer darkness wailing for you in her sleep. She will be covered with dust and cobwebs. She will be surrounded by others sleeping like she sleeps. Or perhaps she will be in a clearing, behind glass like a dead duck in the window of a Chinese restaurant. She will shine like a roasted duck as well. She will be surrounded by little men muttering little words. You will not hear them.

Perhaps the men will be wearing white coats. The shine comes from the sweat on her skin as her fever climbs. She is having no dreams.

Will you recognize her? Her face will be porridge, too hot and too pale, slumped like snow on a fallen scaffolding. Her hair will be pulled back. There will be pallid florescent lights and no color on the beige walls. The floors will be in washed out squares like the floor of your high school. Her high school too. You will sit down next to her and take her hand. She is not there. You can see her. You can touch her. You can smell her. But she is not there. Her chin is hanging in a very peculiar way.

Her eyes are too big and so are her teeth. She is bleeding. She is dying, Egypt, dying. She is dead. She is in chains, long whisper-thin chains. They are as slender as the skein of wool you have unwound as you walked.

Did I not mention the skein of wool?

Do not forget the wool. It is your memories, your time.

The chains are not silver. They are not metal. They do not make a clinkety-clankety clattering noise.

They are pale and fuzzy. They are colorless. They look like dust bunnies stretched out, like gray hairs knit together by dead skin. There are so many of them, they cover your beloved completely and hide her face. She cannot breathe. The dust is in her throat and she cannot breathe.

4. Your Beloved

She is one of many and you cannot find her. You cannot recognize her. Also, you are exhausted. You have come such a long way already.

You will always know her. She is young and she has long blonde hair. She is young and she has cherry-red lips and hair black as the raven's wing. She is old, so old that she is dead, with short white hair almost all fallen out.

She has hair like yours, short and coarse, dark and curly. She wears cats-eye glasses. She is shorter than you are. She has mole in the center of her neck and a scar on her right temple from a cat's scratch.

Cats are never up to any good.

Her fingers are swollen. Her tongue is swollen and chapped, and it has been bleeding.

She has a short tongue.

She is young enough to be your daughter.

She is your daughter.

She is only bones.

Her fingers are swollen. Her rings don't fit any more.

He looks like you, a warrior-king. Lean. Muscles. Scars.

She looks just like you, only she is dead.

5. What you will do

You will kiss her. Everybody knows that.

6. What else

You will kiss her.

You will jar her or perform the Heimlich maneuver. She might be choking on an apple or some pomegranate seeds or maybe a plastic tube. Help her.

Play music. Play her favorite song on your wonder horn. Play a wild tearing song. Play a love song. Play sixty-nine.

Draw the needle out of her arm with your lips. Stop the blood with your mouth. The tube and the needle are not helping any more. And she hates them.

It will hurt. Paint your face now, so that you look like a warrior. There will be snakes crawling beneath your skin. You will vomit from the pain, and because it is disgusting to be filled with snakes.

Lower the guard rail at the side of her bed. Check her hair for poisoned combs. Unsnap the shoulder of her gown.

Lie down next to her very carefully. Wrap your arms around her. She will not hug you back. Rest your head on her shoulder. You will have to go to where she is. Close your eyes. It might hurt. It will hurt.

You can cry. It won't help.

7. Afterwards

She will turn her head and look at you. Call her name. She will recognize you and smile. She is so tired. And she hurts. She hurts so much. She is confused. She doesn't know where she is. She won't thank you. She will blink and sit up.

Take her by the hand. Hold her tightly.

Give her one of your torches.

Don't worry if she doesn't talk at first. Voices take a long time to come back. And anyway, her throat hurts from the tube. Or the apple. The pomegranate. Whatever.

Lead her out. Don't look back.

8. How to Bring Someone Back from the Dead

There is no way to bring someone back from the dead. But you will make the journey anyway.

THE ICE PUZZLE
CATHERYNNE M. VALENTE

In the corner, there are the skeletons of a hundred boys, frozen into art, crystalline and shimmering under their crust of ice.

They make a complicated architecture.

The little skulls glitter coldly like a pilgrim's progress, each smooth lump of bone paler than perfection, ascending towards the light. Ribs arch like drawn bows, pelvises smile, open as communion plates—they do not compete for pride of place, they do not clatter when the wind scours through the hall. They are peaceful, content, complete. And they are silent, as all children should be. They are my opus, my silver sons gleaming with the shell of their afterbirth, the scabrous ice of my body, trailing out of me like a leak of diamonds.

Did you think you were special?

You did, poor, precious thing! You thought you were the only beautiful boy ever to be nestled into my sled, to feel the illicit brush of my nakedness under the white furs, to be marked with the snow-brand of my kiss. They all do, they all want me to be a virgin beneath them, to see my skin break open like a sea choked with sparkling floes, and the black ocean bubble up over their narrow hips. They take my kisses reverently, their tongues quivering as though waiting for the wafer, the transfiguration of bread to woman. And a sweet cake is such a small thing to give, the frosted grace of my lips on their hungry mouths.

It takes the cold away, and my house can be so cold.

The wetness of it froze on your brow, a star of belonging. It is pleasant to recall such things here, under blue rafters and a tight-woven thatch of ice. It was not so very long ago that you climbed into my lap and touched my dazzling cheek with wonder. And even when you have seen the bone-cairn with all those opaline teeth dashed out on the floor, you tilt your head towards mine for another kiss.

There, there, I do love you after all. I love all my sons equally.

You wanted for a mother—that was plain to see. Pawing in your flowerbox with a sallow-braided milkmaid—she was nothing but a doll, a ceramic-faced fetish easily dashed on the surface of a January lake. And no one to look after you but an old, senile hag drooling on her pillow. You were a pretty thing, but you wanted for a mother, for eyes like spinning well-pulleys to draw you out of the tenements, out of geraniums and weak tea, out of dull slashes of rain against filthy windows. It would have been cruel to leave you there, to turn my back on you and tell you that no, I would not show you marvels, not even one.

For you stood on that baroque little balcony with its

wrought-iron lilies and turned your face to the silver sun, the shaded disk behind a sheet of clouds—so like the shade of my flesh!—and you wished to be a man, for that honey-stuck girl-child to look at you and admire, to be suddenly broad and tall as a soldier with his bayonet glinting. I heard your voice like the peal of bells at Mass, begging for your eyes to be changed, to see through a mirror of ice, to be mothered by light. You did not know I was so near, so near! I floated through the snow like white bees swarming, I swelled among them like a queen gorged on jelly, I saw the radiance of your bones like rods of fire within you.

And I was happy to do this for you, to be terrifying—for all proper men dwell in a terror of women. To be forbidden for you, so that the taking of my favors would be sweet as cider. To be the snow-covered forest in which you could lose your way, to be the shadow-curtained bedchamber where you could lose your innocence. I only do as I am asked, after all. It pleased me to be your mother, to make you afraid of me, of the punishments I would visit on your savory flesh, your pale flesh that shows the brilliant shades of bruises, frostbite, and gangrene so well. I was happy to pull you to my breast, to suckle you on the sugar-plum spice of my icy milk, to fold you in my cloak of reindeer pelts and arctic furs, and trace skate-patterns on your pretty neck with my icicle-tongue.

It is what you wanted, is it not?

I put my moon-sliver into your eye like a monocle and gave

you my body to eat, my steaming blood to drink. In a dozen places I have opened my skin to you, tiny throats flooding sweetness into your mouth like a mother pelican. I am an open font, your fingers twisted in my silver-spangled hair like an infant. You put your tiny hands on my sapphire breasts and forgot Denmark, forgot Gerda with her plump pink cheeks, forgot jam and sugar on Sunday morning, forgot the smell of butter melting in a black pot. What were those things but death and death and death; rotting fruit and stale bread, fat sizzling in a smelted pan, flesh speeding toward putrefaction since the hour of its birth. I am life, I am winter, tunnel into me and I will shelter you, ice frozen over ice.

Is it not better here, in my hall of snow-drifts, my towers of spiraling crystal, my altars of antlers and icicles? The breathless light comes fractured through the walls—there is no dawn or meek twilight. See how prettily the water has frozen into buttresses and turrets? Even flags to tip the towers, brazen and clear. For these wonders, would you not trade the heat of your blood? To lie down in a bridal chamber of glass, under a coverlet of netted snowflakes, and close your mouth over my belly? What are fat apples and salted dough, Parliament, bicycles and leather-stitched shoes in comparison?

A boy must be loyal to his mother; he must love her best of all.

Into your hands, still sticky with my milk and kisses, I put these shards of ice and bone. With both hands I give them, toys for my youngest child. Like pearls for a wife, I put these faceted slivers into your pale and purpling hands. They are special, they are secret. Only do as I ask, and I shall give you the whole world, and a new pair of skates. Only do this, and I will score your back with the whips of my white hounds, I will burn your thighs with ropes of ice, and hush the welts with my lips—and I shall do it whenever you wish.

It is a puzzle, my love, a riddle for clever children. Here is a femur, here, a coccyx. Take them, take sternum and collarbone, finger and rib. Take the shards of all my other boys, all my pretty ones, my family, and fit them together to spell a word: *eternity*.

In Danish, naturally. *Evighed, evighed*. A single word, so fragile—yet the world was born from a word. Only do this and I will silence you into art with the rest of them, I will build you into my cathedral, into the catacombs, into the sacred places where holly berries grow. I have made them princes and patriarchs, every one. I have buried them in glacial coffins in sealskin regalia, I have oiled their feet and placed coins on their eyes. I have given them all the proper rights—a mother can do no less.

And I have wakened them again into artifice, into seraphim, free of flesh, marrow-saints arching their wings towards heaven.

Gerda can only offer you her bourgeois womb, squirming with a dozen other Gerdas, and call that the solution to all puzzles of ice and snow. I am eternity, my womb knows the secret tongues, it knows the taste of all my sons, it knows the salt of your tears and your frozen limbs. Show her your proud markings, where I have opened you like a porcelain box. Show her how I have taught your little body to be hard, to be cruel, to be strong. Show her that you are the last shard, and lay yourself into the ice-puzzle, your perfect whiteness gleaming like a revelation. I shall give you the whole world, the heights and the deeps, and the black sea will bubble around you as you sink, as you fall. I will give you the world within me, and let you cut into my stomach with your bright silver skates, let you tattoo my shoulders with your teeth.

Lay yourself into the letters, lay yourself into my snows, my dead trees, my spider-lattice of pure ice. Let Gerda come, let her sing her little song. What can she sing that I have not whispered to you in the night? Let her fish-mouth gape.

Be a good boy. Do as mother says.

Evighed.

SKULL VAULT
SARAH SINGLETON

Tugged from the red clay
Of a sluggish river bed
The skull was fished out,
No flesh,
A bone dish,
A mortar scoured by stones.

Two-thirds river worn,
The rest rich brown of silt and soil,
Where it lay long buried,
A bone cap stuffed with mud.

Skull vault,
Occipital and parietals
Of a young man

Three thousand years dead—
A bowl full of river water.

Ground out, teeth scattered,
Sucked and scraped,

Embedded in moist clay,
Thought, lust and fear long gone.

A cup of life tipped out,
Sop for ungenerous gods
Who wouldn't stint on rain—
The water lying heavy,
Blighting grain.

Now the rain fails—
The river runs thin
And the bed coughs up,
Like old knots in a dry throat,
Skulls dreaming of sunshine.

JOLLY BONNET
ANDREW BONIA

Her new hat
Made of fresh woven straw, and un-scuffed
As she is, (stained red)
Matches the colour of night and street;
Two words that, along with 'woman of the'
Comprise her current circumstance.

Straw, cut down when all is ready
Can be formed into many things
From bread (the yardstick of the civilized)
To feed for beasts.
Or sometimes woven within other strands to make a bed,
A placemat, matching coasters
Or a hat.
Or other trifles I've forgotten.

When last seen, she was heading to work
Head strong and confident in her ability to perform
As though she had discovered a new edge, making her special.
Still, she points at her new hat, black and straw-made
And with a grin that comes from sleeping in the dirt

She opens up and shares her final secret;
"See what a jolly bonnet I've got now?"

Night and Street,
Woven within other strands
Making her special.
Her new hat
In the dirt
(stained red)
Cut down when all is ready
As though she had discovered a new edge.
Night and Street.
Other trifles I've forgotten.

IN GRANDMOTHER'S HOUSE
AINSLEY DICKS

In the midst of the elder trees of the Black Forest, the pinewood house sits as ever it has, though emptier these past few years. The brook whispers, hushed by snow, as it trickles past the doorstep and down into the deeper woods, where the forest is so dense that a man may be lost for weeks without ever once retracing his steps or catching sight of the winter sun. Lost for weeks he may be, indeed, if the wolves do not find him first and make of him their Michaelmas feast.

But from the red-brick chimney of the cottage drifts a wisp of smoky warmth into the frozen sky, and beyond the icy windowpane sits a woman with silvern hair to match the frost. The blaze in the hearth warms the single downstairs room, and, slowly twirling her spindle in one hand, the old woman sings to the muted rhythm of her rocking chair on the sanded pinewood floor, sings to drive the cold winter away.

She sings the berry-picking song of a young girl venturing into the darkling wood, alone with the restfulness of ancient trees and the lure of eider-soft moss, where she dare not sleep an instant, lest she awaken in the company of wilder things.

She sings the wedding song of a young bride, whose head is full of the scent of new pine and who dances on floors strewn with sweet grass in the strong arms that build her a haven against the darkness.

Finally, she hums the lullaby of a young mother, whose darling will all too soon seek comfort beyond her mother's embrace, walking alone into the great woods to forge her own refuge there.

She rocks and sings, she who is a grandmother now, until she falls to coughing, choking on the dry rasp that has come upon her these past few years. As the fit subsides, she stills her spindle and slowly rises, steadying herself against the wooden mantle surmounting the hearth.

The firelight is unsteady as her hands, and, as she stands at the hearthstone, a thought comes upon her, just as a ray of light will oft-times break through the leafy ceiling of the wood to illuminate an ancient tree-stump or a tiny, perfect flower. Her mind slowly awakens like that miniature bloom opening its petals to the unexpected light, and she follows the narrow sunbeam of the thought away from the warm blaze, to a shadowy corner of the modest pinewood room. There, in the nook beside a rack hung with summer's perfumed herbs, is a cupboard whose contents have long been left to hungry moths and darkness.

The cupboard breathes the gentle scent of memory as she opens wide its door, and the old woman pushes aside the loneliness and bone-deep ache of recent times in search of something unremembered from her past. She finds it, buried deep beyond recollection on the cabinet's lowest shelf, between the aroma of her mother's apple-cakes and the wide-eyed thrill of a young girl's first snowfall. Grasping it as firmly as she might with hands grown brittle and weak these past few lonely years, she draws it out from its dusty resting place and holds it close to her.

It is a wolfskin, silvern as her hair and soft as rainfall in a moonlit glen. She presses it to her face and inhales its odor of chill winter nights and secret forest pine-trails, faint but lingering still beneath the must of forgotten decades.

The room is bright with the light of the fire crackling in the hearth, but the warmth of the blaze is oppressive in the tiny pinewood room. Outside the window, night has fallen, and a pale crescent moon is just rising over the forest's frozen treetops. The old woman's skin is cool as the evening, in spite of the heat of the fire, as she looks from her delicate spindle to the waxing moon.

Her little house is warmth on a frigid northern night. It is light in the midst of tree-shrouded gloom. It is aching, yearning emptiness. And the old woman's heart longs for the wilderness.

She glides to the oaken door and, unlatching it, swings it open onto the icy night. The orange firelight that reaches wistfully out over the snow is swallowed by the shadowy trees, which recede into darkness and the unknown. Slowly, fighting the stiffness in her bones, the old woman wraps the skin around herself. Then, her transformation complete, she slinks outside, silent as the snowfall, and slips within the protection of the weald, following the whispering brook into the deeper woods, where the forest is so dense that a man may be lost for weeks without ever once retracing his steps or catching sight of the winter sun. Behind her, the warm light of the pinewood house recedes into the darkness.

She does not return until the first star of morning appears in the lightening sky.

Thenceforth, the old woman rocks in her chair beside the hearth while brief, frozen sunlight fills the small pinewood house, savouring those rare days when her little granddaughter walks the long woodland trail to visit her. But, when dusk settles over the waking forest, she slips into her wolfskin and steals away, disappearing into the night. Days in the wood grow shorter and shorter as the northern winter closes in, and her nighttime wanderings take her further and further afield. Later and later is her return to the pinewood house each morning, until, one day, she does not return at all.

Silence, broken only by the muffled sound of settling snow. The she-wolf's breath rises in steamy tendrils about her mouth, drifting drowsily up into the chill night air as she stands on a knoll in the midst of the trees. All is stillness on this cold winter evening.

The wolf's age has begun to show on her thick coat,

which is silvern and rippling like the ice glazing the whispering brook at her feet, but her legs are steady and swift as she leaps down the hillock and dashes along the slippery riverbank. She has left her pack-mates far behind her in the safety of the deeper forest, and her silken ears prick to their calls as she flies alone through the night. She will enjoy their company nearer dawn, when they will roll and tumble together over the fragile crust of the new-fallen snow before settling into snug earthen dens pregnant with the sharp scent of pine needles.

For now, the she-wolf is content in the stillness of the evening and the speed of her flight. As she rushes on, weaving through underbrush coated in crackling frost, the tall trees begin to thin, almost imperceptibly, withdrawing from each other as though wary of some drowsing menace. The wolf's eyes are sharp, despite her speed, and the gradual change in the forest does not escape her. She slows when the ground takes on a gentle slope and, having crested the modest rise, halts completely.

Before her lies a clearing, sheathed in moonlight. On its open ground, the snow is speckled with the subtle tracks of sparrows and squirrels, and the loping trail of a solitary badger. The meandering brook murmurs its anticipation to a small pinewood house in the midst of the glen before passing by the she-wolf and tumbling on into the deeper woods, back the way she came. The cottage is dark as the night surrounding it, but, amongst the thick trunks of the ancient trees, its tiny frame looks insignificant and lonely.

The wolf lifts her muzzle to sniff the frostbitten air. She did not intend to come this way, yet this place is a familiar one. Wolves lose their teeth, but not their memories.

She watches the moonlit house from the shadows of the woods. The night wind bears no scent of danger, but she is reluctant to leave the haven of the trees. Eventually, though, she steals out from the forest's edge and pads silently across the barren field to the threshold of the pinewood house. The door is slightly ajar, and downy snow has blown in between it and the worn oaken jamb to trace ghostly, sweeping whorls on the uneven floor. She nudges the door open with the tip of her furred nose.

The room beyond is still and musty. When the wolf ventures past the halo of moonlight and snowflakes ringing the doorway, and once her eyes have adjusted to the darkness, she can see a small wooden table to one side of her. Before her, there is a rocking chair, and a hearth. All is covered in a thin film of dust.

The house is peaceful like a den and retains the fresh scent of pine, despite its smell of age and disuse. The wolf glides forward, and tiny puffs of dust well up around her paws as she moves. Pacing out a place for herself, she settles down before the unlit hearth. Her companions will not miss her for just one night. Their memories are long.

She remembers, too, but is not possessive. The tracks she leaves are small, and she will be gone before morning.

She lowers her head and sleeps.

But, cocooned in the sweet scent of pine, the wolf sleeps long past dawn's bright clarion call. Dawn's clarion call does not rouse her, and she does not wake until her dreams are riven by a small, soft sound like the winter wind that chases the frost unceasingly from one end of the forest to the other. The wolf's ears awaken her heavy eyes, which see in the doorway a small shadow, slim and lithe as a young spruce at dusk, silhouetted by the aurora shining beyond the door's oaken threshold. The shadow's dim features resolve themselves into a delicate face, eyes and mouth round as the moon.

It is the she-wolf's little granddaughter—she has not forgotten. The girl's skin is pale snow and her red cloak the luscious berries of the rowan-tree that lie upon it. In her hands she holds a woven basket, covered in a cloth bluer than the sky and flecked with white spots like snowflakes on the breeze.

The wolf smiles her gentlest smile at her beautiful granddaughter. She rises to meet her, shaking the dewy remnants of sleep from her silvern fur, yet, as she approaches, her granddaughter stumbles backward. The young girl's wide eyes are as bright and uncertain as twin candle-flames. Concerned, the she-wolf steps nearer still, but her deliberate stride is interrupted by a sharp intake of breath and the red arc of her granddaughter's arm.

A brilliant white star explodes into luminous being beneath her velvet ear, and her granddaughter's woven basket clatters sorrowfully against the sanded pinewood floor. The she-wolf crumples to the ground, soundless as a falling leaf. Her sensitive ears barely discern the snow-crunching crackle of her granddaughter's receding footsteps before darkness settles over her eyes once more.

When her senses at last return to her, she is alone with the maudlin scent of summer herbs long out of season. The pinewood room has brightened, while she slept, in dull reflection of the sun's ascent into the frozen sky, but, though she longs for the refuge of the shadowed woods, she cannot rise for the lightning storm that plays incessantly about her clouded head.

While she lies awaiting the tempest's misty end, she gradually becomes aware of the sound of voices in the clearing just beyond the doorstep. One is hushed and nervous, the other loud and unnaturally resonant in the still winter air. The voices near the house, and, presently, two figures appear at the door, looming large above her lying prone upon the floor. It is the wolf's young granddaughter, eyes wide and fearful, fragile as a water-lily. Beside her stands a bearded woodsman from the nearer forest, shod in heavy leather boots and bearing in hand an axe that glints in the morning sunlight like long evenings by the hearth. He tells the young girl not to fear, and grasps the dizzy wolf, still too weak to stir, by the velvet scruff around her neck.

He turns the she-wolf onto her furred back and, with a word of caution to the girl, lifts his shining axe above his head.

The wolf is calm, forgiving as the axe falls sharp upon her tender belly. Her granddaughter is green, and the woodsman has no memory. She thinks of the easy companionship of the den and the wild excitement of running before the wind at dawn, of the frozen stillness of a forest glen at night and the chiming music of spruce laden with shimmering ice, as the lustrous wolfskin is stripped from her, revealing a frail old woman with hair as silvern as the frost.

Her granddaughter rushes forward to embrace her, and the old woman silently enfolds the trembling girl in her thin arms. Her wolf's heart has room enough for many things.

The woodsman, his service rendered, tramps off into the snow. He takes with him the ragged wolf pelt, fine fabric for a winter hat or hearth-side rug.

Back in the pinewood house, where pale tendrils of smoke drift once more from the red-brick chimney into the frosty air, the young girl sits her feeble grandmother in the old rocking chair by the fire, and passes her the spindle, and brews her herb-rich tea, and spends all day at her side. But when twilight creeps across the forest like a silken glove, she rises and, bidding her grandmother farewell, sets out along the woodland path for home. Alone, then, the old woman sings softly to herself as she taps a muted rhythm on the sanded floor.

As the years pass in the pinewood house, she grows forgetful like the waning moon, and the cupboard with the scent of memory is buried deep beneath a brocade robe of ash and dust. But, every so often, on a cloudless winter night, her ears prick to the calls of wolves far off in the darkness of the deeper woods.

ALDERLEY EDGE
ELIZABETH WEIN

The red stone slants into bright sand and hard
steep twisted paths below the crooked scarp,
dim cave mouths gasping where old mines have scarred
the dusty cliff face. The tormented, sharp
red wind of drought skitters across the Edge.
The fields and chimneys of the Cheshire plain
seem reeling in the haze; heather and hedge
cling to red sandstone earth and wait for rain.

The oaks and holly hum: "A beacon shone
here when the Spanish ships were threatening.
Armed knights sleep in the caves. And no bird calls
at Castle Rock or from the Golden Stone.
The Wizard's face is carved above the spring;
even in drought the holy water falls."

SHE UNDOES
GREER GILMAN

She undoes her hair,
        unbraiding to the wind
                the bright—it's thin now,
    falling to the comb, November,
cold in coming—bright as leaves
                her hair.
The bone pins bristle;
        she is wrists
    and elbows.
        Knees.
Shy as dryad (virginal),
        the old girl's wild,
            the dark
                    and cloudrush
                          of the sky
    her mind, her nightlong riding
                boneward.
        Bloodrags sail.
                (The moon
    Wanes.)

"Done."
        "Undone."
                "And all to do,"
her sisters cry.
      Her selves. Unselving
            in the dark, the midwood.

Ah, they all go bare
      and they live by the air,
           sings Mally.
In and out her hands, the long swift
      stiffened hands unbraiding
            bear the stars, the seven
                Pleiades her ring.
    Orion is her comb.
The braid's undone.
    She shakes it, falling
        lightloose bright about her,
to her knees, as long
      as to her feet. She stands
          knee deep in dreams.
Unspelled, they scatter.
  A

      and

          O,
    they whirl away.

           No more.
        No matter.
Let them rake at her,
     cries Sibyl with her hands.
And nightlong
     winterlong her owl-
          winged hair's
               unbound.
She will not do it up.

MY SIX MONTHS' DARKNESS
JEANELLE M. FERREIRA

This is all I have to bring you,
finger-spelling on your shoulder,
waiting for my words to come.
A pomegranate only, and
a small one, even if I call it
red-flower echo of last summer's sun.
Please, cut, eat, stain your fingers
redder than kisses, that time you read
Song of Songs to me (years ago
and fading leaf-light, your hair wrapped
me, I heard snow on the sills)
half chanting, in my bed.
You took it from my hand knowing.
Sweet with sour shines on your lips, and I
could hold you here again,
my six months' darkness.

BIOGRAPHIES

A University of Pennsylvania graduate, **Sarah Koplik** is currently pursuing a PhD in Near Eastern Studies at The Johns Hopkins University. In the summers she can be found happily playing in the dirt at one of the many archaeological sites in the Middle East. She is an avid reader of ancient history, mythology, and all types of science fiction and fantasy. "The Mummy Speaks" and "Medea" are her first published works.

Tim Pratt lives in Oakland, California, where he works as an assistant editor and reviewer for *Locus*. He co-edits a zine called *Flytrap* with his fiancee, writer Heather Shaw. His stories and poems have appeared in *Asimov's, Strange Horizons, Realms of Fantasy, The Year's Best Fantasy and Horror, Lady Churchill's Rosebud Wristlet,* and other nice places. His story "Little Gods" was nominated for the 2003 Nebula Award.

Sonya Taaffe has a confirmed addiction to folklore, mythology, dead languages, and all possible combinations of the above. Her short fiction and poetry have appeared in various magazines, including *Not One of Us, Realms of Fantasy, Mythic Delirium, Flytrap,* and *Say . . .*, and her poem "Matlacihuatl's Gift" shared first place for the 2003 Rhysling

Award. A respectable amount of her work has recently been collected in *Singing Innocence and Experience* and *Postcards from the Province of Hyphens* (Prime Books). She is currently pursuing a Ph.D. in Classics at Yale University.

Ekaterina Sedia lives in Southern New Jersey in the company of the best spouse in the world, two emotionally distant cats, two leopard geckos, one paddletail newt, and an indeterminate number of fish. To date, she has survived drowning in the White Sea, standing in front of a moving tank, and graduate school. Her first novel, *According to Crow*, was released in May 2005 from Five Star Books. She has sold short stories to *Analog*, *Aeon*, *Fortean Bureau*, *Lenox Avenue* and the *Poe's Progeny* anthology, among others. Visit **www.ekaterinasedia.com** for more information.

Born in London, England and raised in Toronto, Canada, **Gemma Files'** horror and dark fantasy fiction has appeared in magazines like *Grue, The Vampire's Crypt, TransVersion, Palace Corbie*, as well as in anthologies like *Seductive Spectres, Demon Sex, Northern Frights 2 and 5, Queer Fear I and II, The Year's Best Fantasy and Horror 13,* and *The Mammoth Book of Vampire Stories By Women*. Her story "The Emperor's Old Bones" won an International Horror Guild award for Best Short Fiction of 1999. She is happily married to upcoming high fantasy and science fiction writer

Stephen J. Barringer, has tattoos, a pet snake and very thin skin, and is currently hard at work on a first novel.

Marie Brennan holds a B.A. in archaeology and folklore, and is pursuing a Ph.D. in cultural anthropology and folklore. Between academia and writing, she is waging a losing battle against the size of her library. Her first short story appeared in Julie Czerneda's YA anthology *Summoned to Destiny*; *Doppelganger*, her first novel, is due out from Warner Aspect in spring of 2006.

Mike Allen lives in Roanoke, Va., with his wife Anita, two comical dogs and a demonic cat. He contracted a severe case of the poetry virus in 1994 while working toward his Master's in creative writing at Hollins University. Since then, he's had about 150 poems published in places ranging from *The Pedestal Magazine* to *Asimov's Science Fiction*. His much rarer short stories have appeared in *Flesh & Blood* and *Interzone*. In his spare time, he's both editor of the poetry journal *Mythic Delirium* and president of the Science Fiction Poetry Association. By day he's a newspaper reporter, and was part of a multiple award-winning team that exposed problems with domestic violence cases in his home city.

Yoon Ha Lee's poetry has previously appeared in *Star*Line* and *The Magazine of Speculative Poetry*. She uses her husband, an astrophysics doctoral candidate, shamelessly as a resource, and thinks everyone should have a pet physicist. You can see more of her work on her website, **pegasus.cityofveils.com**, or send her email at **requiescat@cityofveils.com**.

Lila Garrott lives with her wife and seven housemates (counting the two cats) in Cambridge, MA, where she is not actually a graduate student. She has sold fiction to *Not One of Us* and criticism to the *Internet Review of Science Fiction*, as well as (obviously) poetry to *Jabberwocky*.

Holly Phillips currently resides in a crooked old house on a hillside above Trail, BC. She has a fabulous view down the Columbia valley, almost to the point where the river crosses the border into the US, and shares her abode with a whimsical and talkative cat named Savoy. When she is not writing, she is playing music as one third of Pickled Thistle, hiking, reading, preparing workshops, or watching baseball. Holly is presently taking a break from writing short fiction to work on a novel or two. Her first collection, *In the Palace of Repose*, saw publication in early 2005 (Prime).

Shirl Sazynski believes in the pursuit of knowledge and all things beautiful—and an insouicient perception of gender, exploring the history of the beautiful male embraced in Japanese pop culture (**www.bishoneninfo.com**). A student at

Hollins University, she is a regular contributor to *Animerica* magazine, editorial assistant at *Mythic Delirium*—and simultaneously attempting to learn ancient Greek, martial arts and how to play the harp—though not necessarily at the same time.

JoSelle Vanderhooft is a poet, novelist, playwright and freelance journalist currently wandering the United States of America with her computer and two African drums. When not writing, she is thinking of writing. Her first poetry collection, *10,000 Several Doors* will be available from Cat's Eye Publishing in July 2005. She is currently editing an anthology of lesbian fairytales for Torquere Press.

Theodora Goss lives in Boston with her husband and daughter, and the necessary number of cats. She was a lawyer, but decided it just wouldn't do. She is now working on a PhD in English literature. She enjoys introducing unsuspecting freshmen to Lord Dunsany and Philip K. Dick, and needs more bookshelves. Her stories have appeared in *Realms of Fantasy, Polyphony, Alchemy, Lady Churchill's Rosebud Wristlet*, and online at *Strange Horizons* and *Fantastic Metropolis*. Several have been reprinted in *The Year's Best Fantasy* and *The Year's Best Fantasy and Horror*. Her poems have appeared in magazines such as *Mythic Delirium* and *The Lyric*. She has won a Rhysling Award for her speculative poetry.

Vera Nazarian immigrated to the USA from the former USSR as a kid, sold her first story at the age of seventeen, and since then has published numerous works of short fiction in anthologies and magazines such as the *Sword and Sorceress* and *Darkover* series edited by the late Marion Zimmer Bradley, *Talebones, Outside the Box, On-Spec, The Age of Reason,* and *Strange Pleasures* 2. Her work has been translated into seven languages. She made her novelist debut with the critically acclaimed *Dreams of the Compass Rose,* followed by *Lords of Rainbow.* Look for her novella *The Clock King and the Queen of the Hourglass* with an introduction by Charles de Lint from PS Publishing, and first collection *Salt of the Air* with an introduction by Gene Wolfe from Prime Books, 2005. Official website: **www.veranazarian.com**

Rio Le Moignan is from Guernsey, gets on better with her siblings than seems completely normal, and does care work to support her writing habit. Her only previously published poem is online at *Strange Horizons*, and she welcomes visitors to her journal at **www.livejournal/users/apotropaism**

Anna Tambour currently lives in the Australian bush with a large family of other species, including one man. A former industrial designer, her haiku have appeared in various international publications such as *The Red Moon* anthology, and her fiction, in *Strange Horizons, Infinity Plus, The HMS Beagle*, and in *Monterra's Deliciosa & Other Tales &*, her collection of fiction and a bit of poetry. *Spotted Lily,* a novel (Prime, 2005), is also now ready to kill trees for your pleasure.

Catherynne M. Valente is the author of *The Labyrinth* and *Yume no Hon: The Book of Dreams*, as well as two chapbooks of poetry, *Music of a Proto-Suicide* and *Oracles: A Pilgrimage*. Between novels she occasionally moonlights as a literary critic. She currently lives in Virginia with her husband and two dogs.

Stephanie Burgis is an American writer living with her husband (and fellow Clarion West grad) Patrick Samphire and their border collie, Nika, in West Yorkshire, England. Her story "Some Girlfriends Can" appeared in *Strange Horizons,* and her flash fiction "Hide-and-Seek" appeared in *Flytrap* 2. For more on her and her work, see her website at **www.stephanieburgis.co.uk**

[*"Inside the Tower" first appeared in Strange Horizons, 10 January 2005*]

Jane Yolen, whose stories are loved by children and adults all around the world, is the author of over two hundred books, including novels, picture books, story collections, poetry, and nonfiction—leading *Publishers Weekly* to call her "America's own Hans Christian Andersen." Her many magical books include *Briar Rose, Sister Light, Sister Dark,*

White Jenna, *The One-Armed Queen* (for adults); *and Owl Moon, The Faery Flag, Dream Weaver, Neptune Rising, The Devil's Arithmetic*, and the Young Merlin series (for children). Her books have won the Caldecott Medal, the Regina Medal, the Kerlan Award, the Society of Children's Book Writers Award, the Mythopoeic Award, the Daedalus Award, the Christopher Medal, and numerous other honors.

Jane and her husband, David Stemple, divide their time between homes in western Massachusetts and St. Andrews, Scotland.

Veronica Schanoes is a writer and scholar with a particular interest in myths and fairy tales. Her work has appeared in *Lady Churchill's Rosebud Wristlet* and has won the William Carlos Williams Prize from the Academy of American Poets. Raised in New York City, she has been working on her English Ph.D. at the University of Pennsylvania, and is currently living in London.

[*"How To Bring Back Someone From The Dead" first appeared in Postcards from the Voodoo Sex Cult, No. 1, a chapbook published by Mean Girl Click Projects.*]

Sarah Singleton was born in 1966 and was awarded an Honours degree in English at Nottingham University. She qualified as a journalist and works as a reporter for the *Wiltshire Gazette* and *Herald*. Sarah travelled in Europe,

India and Nepal and now lives in Wiltshire with her husband Brian and two young daughters. She has had short stories published in *Interzone, Enigmatic Tales* and *QWF* magazine.

Andrew Bonia was raised in St. John's, Newfoundland, and thanks to the foresight of his mother, was given a healthy diet of Tolkien, Lewis, Brooks and Eddings. His essays, scripts, short fictions and poety have appeared in various and sundry places, including *TickleAce*, the *Borgo Post* and the *Comic World News*. He is currently living in Connecticut with his wonderful wife, where he is finishing work on his first short story collection, entitled *Silverjack*.

Ainsley Dicks has long had a tumultuous but rewarding relationship with literature, mythology, and folklore, and her poetry and prose have previously been published in *Culture Shock* and the *Queen's Feminist Review*. A Newfoundlander born and raised, Ainsley currently resides in Connecticut with her soulmate, Andrew, whilst pursuing a Ph.D. in Assyriology at Yale University. "In Grandmother's House" was awarded the McIlquham Foundation Prize in Literature from Queen's University (2004).

Elizabeth Wein's young adult novels include *The Winter Prince, A Coalition of Lions* and *The Sunbird*, all set in Arthurian Britain and sixth century Ethiopia. The cycle continues in *The*

Lion Hunter and *The Mark of Solomon* (Viking 2006). Elizabeth has short stories forthcoming in Datlow and Windling's *The Coyote Road* anthology and the "Reckless" issue of Michael Cart's *Rush Hour* (Spring 2006). Elizabeth has a PhD in Folklore from the University of Pennsylvania. She lives in Scotland with her husband and two small children, and frequently squanders writing time keeping her pilot's license current. Her web site is **www.elizabethwein.com.**

Greer Gilman's novel, *Moonwise,* won the Crawford Award and was shortlisted for the Tiptree and Mythopoeic Fantasy Awards. "A Crowd of Bone" is one of three linked stories, variations on a winter myth. The first, "Jack Daw's Pack," was a Nebula finalist for 2001, and the subject of a Foundation interview by Michael Swanwick. A sometime forensic librarian, Gilman lives in Cambridge, Massachusetts, and travels in stone circles.

[*"She Undoes" first appeared in Faces of Fantasy, ed. Patti Perret, Tor, 1996).*]

Jeannelle Ferreirra is twice twelve years old, has been writing since she was six, and holds a degree in Creative Writing from Brandeis University. She enjoys listening to stories and swimming off the coast of Massachusetts; she divides her time between her family's farm there and Washington, D.C.

A Verse From Babylon is her first published novel.

Made in the USA
Lexington, KY
05 June 2012